The Plant Hunter's Tale

To Andrew BB

The Plant Hunter's Tale

CAROLINE CASS

With love
Jilly Cooper
xx

QUARTET

First published in 2012 by
Quartet Books Limited
A member of the Namara Group
27 Goodge Street, London W1T 2LD

A catalogue record for this book
is available from the British Library

ISBN   978 0 7043 7278 8

Typeset by Antony Gray
Printed and bound in Great Britain by
T J International, Padstow

1

For Tara and Tasmin

and

in memory of Rullie

Rhododendrons
and camellias, magnolias
and jasmines, conifers and lilies are now
intrinsically woven into the fabric of our garden
landscape. We take these beautiful plants for granted,
giving little thought to who found them, where they came
from and how they arrived here. Many were discovered in
the middle of the nineteenth century by a handful of intrepid
plant hunters, botanists and explorers who ventured into
the wild places of the world. To seek out and bring
back to the west thousands of exotic foreign plants
that would transform gardens forever involved
travelling for many months through remote lands,
often in great danger. The endeavours of these
brave men, whose names are now only
remembered by ardent gardeners and
scholars, inspired this story of
Rullie Montrose,
an adventurous and
passionate plant hunter.

The tree which moves some to tears
of joy is in the eyes of others
only a green thing which
stands in their way.

WILLIAM BLAKE

For as long as he could remember Rullie Montrose had loved trees. It was his belief that a magnificent tree was the finest of all nature's achievements. He observed them with a tenderness other men might reserve for a beautiful woman and he found both strength and solace beneath the giant beeches which dominated the parkland around his childhood home. These venerable friends, many of them nearly two hundred years old, held for him the wisdom and secrets of the ancients.

The year was 1856 and Rullie felt remarkably fortunate. A love of plants was among the various interests he shared with his late father and as a young man he had fallen quite naturally into the study of botany. His native ability proved providential when the family inheritance eventually landed in the lap of his older brother Calder. It enabled him to escape the clutches of both Church and Army, the respectable road down which many second sons reluctantly trudged.

Rullie embarked instead upon an apprenticeship at the Physic Garden at Chelsea, once the best of its kind in Europe. After four years of dismally paid work he gained enough knowledge to pursue his youthful dream to be a plant hunter.

One who travelled far and wide.

Searching for rare botanical specimens.

He was thirty-four, tall and broad-shouldered with hair as pale as wheat and green eyes which changed colour depending on his mood. In looks and temperament he was as unlike his older brother as two siblings could be.

'As different as rook and rooster,' some said.

The two were not close – many years of Calder's jealous and brooding nature had ensured that any links of affection would be ineluctably weakened. His resentment had been constant since the days when he would find his father and ten-year-old brother cocooned together for hours in the library, poring over the latest botanical book.

The library was the core of all Rullie held dear at Ashmore Hall and on drizzly days, when ash-grey clouds swept across the Dorset vales, the lure of reading a finely bound leather book beside the fire proved irresistible. Rain was as reliable as lambing in spring in this small south-western pocket of England where beyond the gates of the house lay the rambling village of Wexton Abbas.

Once in charge Calder cared not a whit what happened to his younger brother who duly accepted his offer of a small thatched cottage, the roof of which constantly leaked, in the grounds of the estate. Like many of his countrymen who never like to be betrayed into unseemly emotion, Rullie maintained a resigned equanimity over the matter.

He lived in the cottage with Charlotte, his wife of four years – the only daughter of a neighbouring squire. A slender woman,

Charlotte had the wild russet hair of a Pre-Raphaelite beauty, small, exquisite hands and cornflower-blue eyes which saw through the merest of pretensions. Their only child, hastily christened Rose, died a day after she was born and was buried at the foot of a large old Cedar of Lebanon in the garden.

After a brief period of mourning Rullie then did what men do best to alleviate their sorrow in such circumstances – he went back to work.

It was a favourable time for Rullie to be a plant hunter. Demand for plants of horticultural and scientific interest was insatiable – in particular those holding exciting commercial prospects. Sprawling on the banks of the River Thames not far from London, the Royal Botanic Gardens at Kew played a crucial role in the growing interest in both exotic and native plants for commercial and amateur gardeners.

Kew owed its existence to Augusta, the Dowager Princess of Wales who in 1759 fulfilled a long-held desire to extend an existing exotic area in Kew Park and create a botanical garden of her own. Widowed at forty, her husband's death from pleurisy and an unfortunate blow to his heart from a cricket ball had been much lamented by the country's gardening fraternity who declared solemnly that: 'Planting and Botany in England would be the poorer for his Passing.' Nearly a century later, much enlarged and improved, Kew was given to the nation and the renowned botanist Sir William Hooker was taken on board as its first director. It gradually became one of the plant world's great treasure chests.

Sir William was the obvious man for Rullie to approach for help in funding his costly plant-hunting expeditions. A firm friendship was quickly established and an amicable and mutually favourable agreement struck. In return for financial assistance Kew would be suitably rewarded. For every seedling, cutting or packet of seeds found or purchased abroad, half would be allocated for them. Hooker, impressed with the younger man's botanical knowledge and eye for a good plant, told him:

'You have the better bargain, my friend. You get to travel far afield and see the marvels of the world. Bring me back a ravishing plant distinguished by its rarity and it might just make your fortune.'

Most of the remaining plants Rullie sold to a variety of buyers. At the top of his list was the firm of Veitch, the dominant nurserymen of the day, who were only too pleased to pay a thousand pounds for a bag of promising seeds. Other interested parties included private collectors and arboreta, the Horticultural Society of London and the Botanic Gardens at Edinburgh and Oxford.

The rest he kept for himself.

Over the years Rullie had travelled the equivalent of five times round the globe. Setting out in early spring each year he was precise in spending no more than six months away and for much of that time the rainforests, rivers, mountains and valleys of the world became his home. It could be said of him that he was prepared to sacrifice the comforts of home and a charming wife for limitless adventure, but it was a demanding, lonely way of life, unlikely to appeal to those with less than robust fortitude. Fighting off brigands became par for the course and on a recent trip to Chile to collect seeds of the strange monkey puzzle tree – then all the rage in England – he had narrowly missed being scalped by a family of Arauco Indians. There were days he went hungry, existing solely on roots and berries. Fevers and leech bites, accidents and disease all came with the job.

Coming from England, a land which had long ago lost its wilderness and where every rood of land depended for its survival and benefit on man's involvement, Rullie felt a certain exhilaration in being embraced by the throbbing, frenzied abundance of plant life in the tropics. It suited him to be in places where the chorus of frogs and cicadas comforted the night and the morning air lay still, watchful, under a sweating sun.

It was his habit, if possible, to be back home by the third week in October, in time to enjoy the last of the autumn colour. He usually arrived before twilight, as the last of the swallows flew overhead on their way to warmer lands.

On returning from his trips, it was Rullie's custom to share a few pints of ale with his friend Jamie MacLellan. They met in the village tavern, The Friar's Tuck, each Thursday at seven o'clock. Rullie had recently returned from the mountains of Persia for the firm of Veitch with two crates of chestnut-leaved oak seedlings and was looking forward to spending the next few hours in his company.

MacLellan, the owner of a concern which produced planking timber for building merchant ships, was a titan of a man whose equally large personality was tempered with a fine generosity. His fortunes had risen rapidly after studying forestry in his native Scotland. Having started on his path to success he managed to acquire a wife who would tolerate his romantic encounters and subsume her individuality in the breeding of many children. MacLellan charmed princes, peasants and women with the same easy, cheerful manner.

Amid the smoky atmosphere of the tavern, while strong ale loosened the tongues of men around them, the two friends talked about their travels and derring-do. The image of the Scotsman's narrow escape from an enraged bear deep in a Russian timber forest provoked a few chuckles. Eventually discussions turned to matters concerning Wexton Abbas, in particular Rullie's introduction of a young arboretum, now in its fourth year, into the manicured grounds of Ashmore. By laying out a botanical garden devoted to trees he hoped to create a lasting reflection of what he felt for the natural world, the dream of many men strongly attached to their land.

'However demanding, trees are the seed of our history, the root of our past. They give us warmth and shelter, light and beauty,' he said as he gazed into the flames leaping from the large log fire. 'Don't you agree we should always cherish them?'

Sitting opposite him in a large leather chair, MacLellan nodded from time to time and sucked on his pipe as he listened to the rising excitement in the younger man's voice. For more than an hour, barely pausing for breath, Rullie spoke of his continual need to snare and possess the world's most unusual specimens of trees and plants. Originality, in itself, was not sufficient. They had to be aesthetically pleasing, beautiful, exotic. When he eventually finished, he said in a quiet voice: 'With hard work, by the end of my life I hope it will become one of the wonders of the whole country.'

MacLellan smiled. 'Beware of it becoming your only life.'

As he swilled the last drops from his tankard, his eyes twinkling, he added, 'However, should you wish to take advantage of a rumour I once heard on my own travels in Persia, the rarest flowering plant of all grows in a valley near Hunza.'

Rullie was silent for a minute. He gazed intently at MacLellan.

'I have never heard of the place. Tell me, where would I find it?'

'Nestling at the foot of the tallest mountains in all the world.'

'And what is the name of the flower?'

'Ah, that I do not know.'

17

Rullie remembered the day, soon after the death of his father, when he had broached the subject of the arboretum with Calder, without whose permission the idea would be doomed. He had waited for the right moment, out strolling together in the park one day.

'Just imagine it. We could add maples from Japan, magnolias from the Himalayas, rhododendrons of every size and colour.' His brother continued walking in silence with his hands clasped behind his back, a sudden flash of interest in his dark eyes lighting up his sullen expression.

'It will be magnificent,' Rullie continued enthusiastically, flinging his arms wide as if to embrace his vision, 'American tulip trees cradling five thousand blossoms will eventually burst a hundred feet into the skies.'

Though his sibling was not one to proffer brotherly advice or concern, Rullie had been agreeably surprised when once back in his brother's study he was offered a small yearly stipend with a strict proviso.

'Of course, the project is unlikely to reach maturity in our lifetime and will cost a pretty penny. I must insist that not a solitary farthing is to be spent on anything other than the task of purchasing and planting, beautifying and maintenance,' said Calder.

'That's fine by me,' Rullie hurriedly agreed before his brother could have a chance to change his mind.

A further stipulation was the firm intention to charge a

halfpenny to visitors in future years once the trees had taken firm root and flowering varieties began to blossom. Out of necessity a fair proportion of the money would be given for the project immediately.

'What if the amount does not cover the cost in years to come?' asked Rullie.

'Well, that's your problem, not mine,' his brother replied coolly, his thick black mop of hair obscuring his face as he turned towards the window. He had already brushed the subject away.

That was how it was between them.

Rullie had hired forty hands to help prepare the land late that spring. In those days the village of Wexton Abbas was a place where scattered sheep grazed at its edges and time slipped by hazily. It was filled with country people whose patterns and beliefs were steeped in tradition. Theirs was an arduous life and many, grateful for a few extra pounds in their pockets, were excited at the prospect.

Thickets of elder and brambles were cleared and small hills were levelled. The men worked around the limes, larches, sweet chestnut and beeches whose canopies filled the sky like giant umbrellas. These were left untouched, ready to mingle with the newcomers. All summer long the sound of axe upon wood and spade shifting earth blended with the murmur of bees and the clip-clopping of horses transporting the native trees and shrubs needed. To protect the area from marauding cows grazing in the fields beyond, a hedge would be added in winter – a tapestry of hawthorn and hazel interwoven with holly. After five months the heavy work was over. By early autumn the last of the labourers doffed his hat and walked down the tree-lined driveway back to the village.

The time had arrived for Rullie to sit down with Gibbes, his indispensable head gardener, who had worked diligently on the estate since the age of seventeen, and choose the positioning of each exotic species he had decided upon. Few could fail to be impressed by the blend of planning and energy that went into the venture. Those who knew him well said they had never seen him so happy. But, not disposed to reflecting at length upon the vagaries of the human heart, Rullie held the view that happiness was purely momentary. A rare and unpredictable instant, like retaining upon awakening the face of a past love seen in a dream.

Little by little, as the young arboretum grew plumper, the trees taller and the colours more varied, Charlotte Montrose felt herself drawn to its sympathetic intimacy. Its mysteries, like the moon's, were felt rather than understood. In time she took a quiet delight in camellias as bright as jewels, and since they had a particularly feminine quality to them she liked to walk among the saplings of silver birch and feel the texture of their peeling bark. Being amongst the silent trees helped sooth the sadness of losing her child.

As is common between a couple married for some years, her understanding of her husband's moods had become instinctive, almost perfunctory. In the long months before winter seeped slowly into spring each year, a restless energy sprang from him. A certain emotional detachment. She accepted that in the coming weeks his every thought would be fixed on his imminent venture. It was if his mind, unable to wait for his physical body, had already arrived at its destination.

Soon he would be leaving her again. This time for India.

It was always the same. She would try to ignore the tight knot forming inside her at the thought of yet another separation.

'I shall miss him so,' she murmured to herself.

During the heady days of colonial expansion when young English bloods with a love of independence and talent for commerce were eager for new adventures, Jamie MacLellan had leapt at the chance ten years previously to have his ideas of the world stretched and challenged. He spent a year near the banks of the Swat River, beneath the shadows of the Hindu Kush and the Karakoram. Much of his time was spent honing his forestry skills deep in the sweet-smelling deodar forests which grew below the snow-capped mountains.

In the same year of 1856 when Rullie was about to leave for a land where the British Empire was still busy fulfilling its ambitions, Charles Dickens was at home in London still mulling over his writings of *Little Dorrit*. Further afield the Crimean War was in its death throes and Florence Nightingale would soon be travelling home to create the nursing profession. No one could possibly imagine that such a singular woman would retire to bed for the next twenty years of her life.

Although MacLellan never failed to encourage the enthusiasms of younger men like Rullie Montrose, the concern which now lay closest to his heart was the prosperity of Wexton Abbas, quietly enfolded in its country pursuits, and the welfare of its inhabitants, most of whom he knew well.

It was in his nature to help people.

As the day of the winter solstice drew to a close he learned that his friend had agreed, with his usual speed, to Kew's request to visit the Himalayas. Rhododendrons were the current obsession in the country and Rullie had been asked to seek out a giant specimen growing in the foothills which reputedly grew to a height of more than fifty feet and spilled over with clusters of blood-red flowers. At their meeting Sir William had come straight to the point.

'It's important, Montrose, that you organise your departure promptly, in order to assure territorial advantage over the valleys in question. Before they can be harvested by rival collectors,' he said crisply.

Rullie could barely wait to tell MacLellan his news.

'What a bonanza should I find it. Who knows what else I might come across if I have the time to continue north?' he teased.

Though confident that his friend's ambitions seldom exceeded his valour, MacLellan felt troubled about the proposed trip. He understood the reason for his exuberant state – one of almost missionary fervour if truth be told. It had been a while since he first mentioned the flowering plant of Hunza and in all honesty he had, until now, forgotten all about it. Certainly, never for a moment had he considered that his words, said partly in jest, would be acted upon.

Late one night at home, after one too many glasses of port had somewhat dampened his usual optimism, he said to his old friend Gibbes, 'I employ many labourers from the village. Work on the arboretum will also provide an income for them for years to come. I will continue to do my bit, but what if Montrose goes off on this hair-brained journey of his and never returns?'

MacLellan did not keep these sentiments from Rullie for long.

At seven o'clock on one cold January night the two friends were sitting as usual in front of the blazing log fire in The Friar's Tuck, warming their hands.

'You realise, of course, that Hunza has a bloody, disreputable history,' MacLellan said as he stared into the flames. 'The men may have a great reputation for courage, but they are scoundrels; a rapacious lot. Most of the Mirs come to rule by murdering their father and brothers – the valley's age-old custom.'

'Never mind the cut-throat stuff, Jamie,' murmured Rullie , smiling.

Without really hearing him the Scotsman continued, as if he was on some vivid, all-consuming adventure of his own: 'They survive on the spoils from years of plunder – raiding caravans between Kashgar and Kashmir is a breeze when you live near the old Silk Road. What's more,' he observed, a slight edge to his voice, 'slave trading is one of their favourite pastimes. You'll never get past them. Not a Chinaman's chance.'

The years had brought Rullie confidence rather than wisdom. Had he been asked, he would have answered that wisdom surely lay in rising above the everyday, the mundane; small, sharp disappointments. He tried his best to reassure his friend: 'You know me well enough. I am not inclined to panic.'

MacLellan sighed. 'Well, I will just warn you, Rullie – danger will never be far behind you in the tribal areas. Catch a man on the wrong footing and before you know it your throat has been slit from ear to ear.'

The tavern owner, Symonds, eager to miss nothing of their discussion, was slower than usual in removing their tankards and felt compelled to blurt out,

'Damn it, MacLellan, a man must have new adventures. We don't want him to leave this earth with endless regrets, do we?'

Symonds had known Rullie since he was knee-high to a grasshopper.

If there was one thing upon which the villagers agreed, it was that Rullie was of a singular mind. His plans were seldom thwarted, so calmly and persuasively were his ideas argued. Early the next morning he summoned Gibbes and told him of the tallest mountains in all the world and what he hoped to find there. Under the head gardener's deft direction the arboretum had gradually been filled with all manner of foreign trees. From California came a Wellingtonia, a fir as heroic as its namesake, the recently deceased Duke of Wellington – whose seedlings had cost two guineas a piece; a sharp-smelling eucalyptus; a rare flowering magnolia; a Chinese ginko with plump leaves that clung together like clusters of bright green scarabs. In his employer's absence all agreed there was no one more capable of safeguarding his arboreal interests.

Rullie's departure was, as usual, unassuming. MacLellan gave him two letters of introduction: one to an Englishman in Simla, well versed in Hunza lore and rumoured to have been conceived under a Banyan tree after a regimental ball; the other to an Indian merchant in Swat.

The afternoon before he left, Charlotte and her husband took their customary walk around the garden, discussing in detail the numerous things to be done in the coming months while he was away. For some time the couple observed in silence the purple and white crocuses carpeting the banks of the brook which meandered near the cottage. Both focused on anything but the difficulty of so long a separation.

That night Rullie held his wife closely in his arms.

'I will come back as soon as I can,' he quietly assured her, as he stroked her long russet hair.

In the first week of March as the dawn gathered in the stars, Rullie set out alone and travelled south to the ocean. Among his belongings were two hundred pounds in gold hidden in a leather case, a compass, a map of India and a small flask of whisky. He boarded a ship bound for Bombay and, after travelling the length of Africa, rounded the Cape of Good Hope in a storm which reduced most of the bilious passengers to a state of inertia. They stopped for two days in Zanzibar – a place that signified all that was exotic and malevolent, where the boat's hull was filled with ivory and cloves. To while away the time Rullie spent his days meeting local sheikhs and exploring the twisting maze of coral streets which lipped the lagoon.

Although India considered Queen Victoria, the Empress of India, and their colonial rulers just as alien an occupier as the Mughal emperors before them, the English laid the foundations of their power so deeply that it was obvious nothing less than a moral crusade would oust them. Discussions at the ship captain's table each evening naturally veered towards the country that most of the passengers were to see for the first time. The chosen few at his table soon became accustomed to his lengthy monologues.

'We may be separated by the ocean, by seas, by deserts,' said the captain puffing up with pride one night, 'but it is satisfying to think that no country is more firmly clasped in England's tentacles than the sub-continent, don't you agree?'

Most Englishmen remained unperturbed that the East India Company, with Parliament's consent, had the unusual distinction of ruling an entire country. It set a strict reign of law and order, reaped enormous profits from cheap materials and labour, and exported opium to China despite the ban on it. Although it was true a handful of nawabs were keener on nautch-girls and cockfighting than ruling over their minions, many Indians were dismayed that so many of their princely houses were being deprived of their territories and powers.

As the new governor-general left London for Calcutta that year, the Queen told him fervently, 'Look after my poor Indians.'

She had a soft spot for the people of a land she had never set eyes on, and an interest in the fate of their country lay particularly close to her heart.

But a large number of her subjects were fed up with low pay and livelihoods ruined when all manner of goods from Britain flooded their markets. Their simmering anger at religious indifference and the perilious plight of the peasantry ensured that many of them were growing increasingly resentful at living in the shadow of their foreign masters.

Two thousand miles and thirty-nine days after leaving home, Rullie sailed out of the deep indigo waters of the Indian Ocean and into the Arabian Sea which hugged the western shores of India. From Bombay he travelled a short distance on the new-fangled railway and then by palanquin and horse to the old Mughal capital of Delhi. The land through which he travelled seemed timeless, almost biblical – the sacred animal and camels, the robed travellers and pilgrims, all jostling together along the same dusty roads. After taking a few days' rest he continued his journey, crossing through the sunburnt lands of the Punjab until he reached Simla. Here, nestled in the foothills of the tallest mountains in all the world, amidst green slopes covered with pine, rhododendron and Himalayan oak, the English had built the nearest thing they could to a small town at home. It was their summer capital – a refuge for the sahibs and their families from the gruelling heat of the plains.

Rullie soon found the small bungalow belonging to Charles Cordell, one of MacLellan's contacts, who invited him to stay. A rugged individual, Cordell turned out to be one of the many British agents posing as scholars and explorers, merchants and Muslim holy men participating in England's imperial sabre-rattling with Russia over Afghanistan.

'Our rivals call it the 'Tournament of Shadows',' Cordell explained to his guest over dinner. 'We spend our days criss-crossing and mapping the mountains, spying on each other and courting local rulers. It's an amusing business.'

But English domination and politics held little interest for Rullie. He found himself instead intrigued by the curious tales of Hunza spun by his host as they sat outside later, gazing at the sliver of moon hanging over the mountains. The stories were so full of the unusual, the exotic, the surreal, that they only fuelled his desire to reach the kingdom.

After two days Rullie said goodbye to Cordell and departed on his journey, three hundred miles across the province of Kashmir to Rawalpindi. Once there, he purchased a horse and a mule to carry plants, studied his map, set a route by compass and rode north alone. As he travelled he gathered what material he could from trees which covered that part of the world – chinar, camphor and podcarpus, spruce and drooping juniper. He found it comforting to sit in their shade after an arduous climb and tackle the required pages of field notes, a detailed process requiring an accurate eye and precision drawing. Within ten days he reached the valley of Swat and dined with the Indian merchant who secured a guide and two native collectors to take him on foot further into the mountains. The sharply pungent smell of cedar enfolded the darkening woods and families of small flying squirrels filtered through the forest canopy.

Paths were hacked through the thick undergrowth and each day Rullie climbed for many hours without tiring. After two weeks of searching among the deodars where he came across wild orchids and shy musk deer, he suddenly chanced upon four spectacular rhododendrons. They spilled over with bell-like clusters of deep red flowers, scented and waxy. Towering above the undergrowth, amid the ferns and mosses, the brilliant flowering trees lit up the surrounding darkness. Most importantly, and much to his delight, he found them un-disturbed by other plant hunters. He carefully pressed blossoms and leaves to dry between pieces of fine paper which he placed in a slim leather case. Unable to speak the hill villagers' language, he negotiated the price of the fruits enclosing the seeds by counting on the fingers of his right hand. He would collect these on his return journey once the flowering was spent, and fill his saddle bags with roots and ripe cuttings.

Leaving his helpers behind in the village, Rullie continued his journey north-eastwards towards the higher recesses of the Himalayas, past undulating snow-fields and across glaciers of green ice that glittered in the sun. He forded the Indus river on a raft of blown-up goatskins, skirted the great mountain of Nanga Parbat, entered the desolate, shattered landscape of the Karakorams and eventually reached the village of Gilgit, where he rested.

Beyond him, near the border with China, in a region where few if any foreigners travelled, lay Hunza.

Isolated and majestic.

Rullie was less than an hour's journey from the small kingdom and surrounded on all sides by a labyrinth of mountains. It was a wondrous place. To his east lay ridge upon ridge of white peaks like a tented world suspended in ice. Soaring from its centre was Rakaposhi, a snow-covered mountain of such ethereal grandeur that Rullie felt certain he had arrived at the most beautiful place on earth.

Climbing up a steep narrow path, his hill pony gripping the slippery rocks, he passed women and children who shyly smiled at him. He noticed their eyes were ringed with the dark colour used as a protective measure against the capricious spirits of the sky which crowded the highest peaks and passes – Cordell's stories of the shamans' world of magic, of spells and enchantments, still lingered in his mind. As he continued walking the sound of a flute being played in a ravine below drifted towards him on a flutter of air. He turned and followed the music towards the wisps of smoke which slowly spiralled upwards, seeking a path through the dark blue gorge.

Mist still hung heavy in the early morning. There near an icy stream he found an old man with skin like parchment sitting cross-legged by a fire. In his hands he held a wooden flute with metal trim similar to those sold in the bazaars in Peshawar. A meagre cloak was wrapped around his thin body. Beside him in the base of a large fir he had built a hut out of broken branches. The gnarled roots of the tree, spreading out like giant lion's paws, enveloped the diminutive dwelling.

The woodland setting offered an exquisite solitude. Without missing a note the old man peered at the intruder from eyes which had clearly seen many hardships. He appeared not to mind as Rullie quietly tethered his pony and sat on a boulder on the opposite side of the fire, as though he had been waiting for this visit for all eternity. Not a word was spoken. There flowed between the two men an immediate understanding, as sometimes happens in life. It was if by sitting thus in silence together they might discover the secrets of the earth.

As a stream of sunlight flickered across the ravine floor, the peace was suddenly broken by a clattering of hooves. Into the midst of the clearing six mounted men dressed in robes as black as monks' cowls arrived, matchlocks slung over their backs. While the leading horse pawed the ground, its hooded rider, face partly in shadow, looked long and hard at the foreigner. Holding the silver handle of his whip, he pointed with a flinty authority towards a stone and timber fortress perched like an eagle's nest high on the mountain opposite. Rullie, feeling a sudden twinge of unease, was in no doubt that he was obliged to follow him there.

'Mir Zafran Khan,' rasped the old man, as he resumed his playing.

The heavy wooden doors of Baltit Fort clanged loudly behind him. Following the men across the empty courtyard, he was taken to a dark, cold windowless room of sun-dried mud which he took to be a prison. The only sound that reached him was the tinkling of a thousand bells in the strong wind outside. He waited until a guard arrived and led him to where Zafran Khan was seated on a raised dais in the middle of what appeared to be a large hall with many doors.

The Mir's hunting robes had been removed, exposing a handsomely embroidered coat of the finest weave which was fastened by an elaborate silver belt. Within the chiselled rock of his face he regarded the world from behind heavy eyebrows knitted into one. A neatly trimmed beard covered the lower part of his face. His only other concession to finery was a silk turban, beneath which long black hair hung in knotted ringlets on his cheeks. There was about this huge man a hypnotic quality, powerful and imperious. His hands were pressed together, in a position of prayer.

'Asalaam Alaikum,' he said in greeting. His penetrating eyes, the colour of cold steel, never left Rullie's face.

On either side of the dais, as if it were the most natural thing in the world, lay two snow-leopards tethered by heavy chains. Having been signalled to sit, Rullie sat cross-legged on the floor, his eyes flickering between ruler and animals.

The Mir began to speak in a strange language that was neither Urdu nor Hindi. His voice was cool, dispassionate, gravelly.

Silence fell.

Zafran Khan let it hang in the air for a moment before asking, 'Why have you come to Hunza?' Each word was said haltingly in English, as if being read with the utmost concentration from a child's book.

Before Rullie could answer, a door opened and into the room stepped a young girl, with almond-shaped eyes, almost golden, and loose hair reaching below the small of her back. She wore a garment of the palest green which floated like gossamer as she walked across the floor. From the crown of her head a veil, which did little to conceal her delicate features, was swept back over her shoulders. Behind the quiet demeanour lay a promise of gentleness. For an instant, as he glanced at her, Rullie's breath was snatched away.

On reaching the dais the girl offered Zafran Khan a small brass bowl filled with water and rose petals. He gave a fleeting nod of recognition as he slowly and methodically dipped his hands in the scented water. She then turned towards the visitor and knelt silently before him. With lowered eyes and quick, gentle movements she placed the same bowl under his hands, the tips of her fingers barely brushing his as they slid into the water. The faint scent of a flower he could not name lingered in the air around her. Just as swiftly she rose, made a small gesture of obeisance and vanished.

'One of my daughters,' said Zafran Khan in a matter-of-fact way. 'I am still waiting for your answer. Again I ask, what is your reason for being here?'

Rullie hesitated a moment before replying. It was doubtful the Mir could comprehend the strange, sedulous ways of a wandering Englishman and even less appreciate his addiction to all things arboreal. But since he had encountered only a handful of people to engage in conversation over the past weeks he gradually found no difficulty in talking. Slowly, clearly, he spoke of the vicissitudes of his journey, his gypsy wanderlust and the small truths of his life. By doing so he dared to hope Zafran Khan might recognise the yearning, romantic and insatiable, which lay in his heart, to travel to wild, deserted places where few others have been.

It was only as he reached an almost euphoric state of mind, induced, he supposed, by the rarefied mountain air and the dream-like situation in which he found himself, that he was able to summon the nerve to speak of his quest: 'I have come to find the rarest flowering plant of all. I am told it grows here in your land.'

Zafran Khan had been listening to the foreigner's narrative with hooded eyes half closed, his person as motionless as a temple deity. As he unfolded his arms and reached over to slowly stroke one of the sleeping snow-leopards, as one might a harmless lap-dog, he said curtly, 'You are mistaken. We have no such plants here.'

Rullie was careful not to betray the slightest hint of surprise. Over the years he had grown accustomed to lands which jealously guarded their mysteries, their essential differences. In those places he had found answers only through an unwavering patience. As he pondered upon what line of questioning would least provoke his host, he became aware of a gentle presence behind him, like a soft breeze on the back of his neck. Feeling it discourteous to turn round, he kept his eyes firmly fixed on Zafran Khan as a small dainty pair of silken slippers glided past him.

This time the young girl was accompanied by a servant who carried a large salver of apricots. These staples were carefully dried by the villagers on the roofs of their houses each autumn. In silence the fruit was placed on a small table in front of the dais. Instead of leaving, as he expected, the young girl stayed, sitting on a cushion in the shadows behind her father, the folds of her light green dress falling softly about her. Rullie, used to women of her faith vanishing into their separate quarters on the arrival of strangers, found this unusual.

Unable to resist, he took his gaze off Zafran Khan for the merest of seconds and noticed she had brought a companion. Perched on her left wrist was a small bird, the colour of amethyst. Around its neck, on a ribbon of silk, lay a tiny silver bell which tinkled as its head darted to and fro. Rullie had never seen such a bird before. After accepting offerings of the sweetest apricots he had ever tasted, he resumed talking, thinking it best to leave the topic of the flowering plant to another time – assuming there would be one. In the quiet of the cavernous room he sensed a hypnotic stillness on the far side of Zafran Khan.

The small figure continued to sit motionless, silent, the only visible movement being the occasional fluttering of wings. Her presence, though charmingly composed, disturbed Rullie and he found it difficult to concentrate on the precision of his words. She appeared to be listening closely to the sounds of his language, the neutral cadence of his voice without, he was certain, understanding a single word. As his eyes strayed briefly into the shadows, he glimpsed her tilting her head as she smoothed her bird's feathers. Aware of the Mir's fierce scrutiny, Rullie felt rather than saw her almond-shaped eyes glancing up at him from beneath a stray lock of hair. He felt her gaze like a caress, filled with unexpected curiosity.

'Follow me,' said Zafran Khan, adjusting his turban as he rose. He stepped down and strode towards the door, his thick embroidered coat swinging behind him like a pendulum. As Rullie advanced after him, he felt again the young girl's observation moving over him like a gentle rainstorm. He lengthened his stride to catch up with his host and as he looked back at her, their eyes locking briefly, the faintest of smiles at once both shy and provocative lifted up the corners of her lips.

The two men went back through the dark building, one behind the other. They passed several rooms with wooden pillars carved in an oriental pattern which appeared largely empty, their roofs blackened by the smoke of ages. The sound of soft laughter from the women's quarters rippled on the wind as they stepped onto the uneven stones of a terrace. Below them village houses clung to the mountainside like bats to the roof of a cave. Zafran Khan walked to the edge, where he stood alone. He gazed out over the terraced and cultivated fields, which stretched for seven miles up and down the valley, towards the grey-brown scree slopes of the mountains opposite and beyond to Rakaposhi, just as his ancestors had done from the same spot for the past six hundred years. As if contemplating for a moment the insignificance of time. Only when the lilting cry of the muezzin's voice shattered his reverie, did he break his silence: 'Allahu Akbar.'

He knelt onto a small prayer mat facing west and bowed his head to the ground in homage to his God. As he did so Rullie

42

noticed for the first time the dearth of minarets in the small town and far below, the women working unveiled beside men in the fields. It was clear the people of Hunza felt no need to hide their women away.

When he had finished his brief devotions, the Mir rose and beckoned to Rullie.

They left the fortress and continued down a steep path until they reached an area enclosing a tiered orchard. A fragrant breeze sighed through the poplar trees which lined the fields of young wheat shoots growing by the stream below. Inside the rough-walled field, in ten rows of equal distance, were planted a hundred and sixty apricot trees, covered in swaying blossom of such profusion it seemed as if clouds of white butterflies had settled on each bough. 'These are the most precious trees in my kingdom,' stated Zafran Khan, letting the petals drift through his fingers time and time again, as though he enjoyed nothing more than turning the arrival of spring into a game.

'They produce thousands of small, round, perfect apricots. You can find them nowhere else in the world.'

As they walked, Zafran Khan began to tell a story that belonged to many centuries past. His deep voice oscillated between truculence and a curious detachment.

Hesitating when he came to a word which proved difficult to pronounce in English, he spoke of the hatred between twin princes since infancy who, as kings of Hunza and its opposite village of Nagar, frequently led their people into battle against each other. Royal descendants intermarried and, fuelled by jealousy and distrust, continued the senseless feud.

'Only one daughter escaped the final onslaught.'

The Mir shrugged nonchalantly as he continued with his tale: 'Our ministers, the *'Wazirs'*, desperate to save the royal bloodline, wandered for seven years in search of lost relatives, until guided to Afghanistan by a white crow. A distant cousin was brought back to marry the girl from whom I am descended.' Zafran Khan paused.

'It was from that time the fruit in the valley was grown,' he concluded before falling silent, lost in his thoughts of a realm beyond reach.

As the two men reached the last row of trees, the Mir stopped and said, 'My apricots are famous for their sweetness, but the seeds are never taken out of the kingdom without my consent. Anyone caught stealing them dies.'

Silence.

44

As he looked at the inflexible expression of his host Rullie wondered, 'Who would trifle with the tyrannies of an obscure mountain king?'

They retraced their steps through the orchard, the Mir making no effort to converse but stopping occasionally to inspect a particular tree. Then without any warning, a flicker of a smile passed over his face, as if he had suddenly seized upon a novel idea.

'Since you have travelled for many months from the other side of the world and have been disappointed in your reason for coming here, I will take pity on you. I will allow you four of my treasured seedlings. Only four. One in the name of each of my daughters.'

'That is most generous of you,' Rullie said, thanking him more out of politeness than gratitude. He was not really looking for fruit trees, however exceptional, but for something which, from Jamie MacLellan's account, touched on the sublime.

'In exchange, you will give me all your gold, which I would have taken from you one way or another. Should the plants survive and you return next year with more gold, again you will be rewarded.'

'What guarantee do I have of leaving your kingdom alive if I carry these seedlings?' asked Rullie.

'Insh'allah. That is in God's hands. But if it is so, you and I, we have a bargain,' Zafran Khan chuckled, shaking his head from side to side as affirmation, in the manner of his countrymen.

At first light, Rullie placed the four apricot seedlings in his Wardian Case, a sealed glass case recently invented by a London physician which had forever changed the face of plant collecting abroad. He had been studying a hawk moth chrysalis on a leaf mould in a glass jar and sealed the lid. No moth emerged but instead a tiny fern and a few seedlings sprouted on the moist leaf. On a grander scale it preserved plants in earth and water from wind and salt spray, rats and dehydration during their hazardous voyages home across the ocean. Collectors were eternally grateful to the good doctor for his miraculous device. They could now heave a sigh of relief: that is, assuming their plants survived their inland journey to the coast and the boats did not sink.

Rullie left the mountain fastness without mishap and, after slowly crossing the roof of the world, over its cold, spiny ridges covered in cloud and deep canyons dotted with lonely villages, he managed to retrace his steps to the forest in Swat. There, having hidden a few gold pieces upon his person, he paid for and collected the fruits and cuttings of the rhododendron plants. He then continued south to the Botanic Gardens at Saharanpur in the Punjab, the base for all plant-hunting expeditions, where he purchased seeds of both the India Coral Tree for Kew and the Neem tree, renowned for its medicinal properties. Once in Bombay he boarded a ship full of civil servants bound for home leave in England. Among the numerous plant seeds in the hold, their roots carefully nurtured by a wrapping of soil, were clusters of rare Himalayan primulas, intended as a present for his wife.

In the languid days of sea travel, on ships that steamed slowly across the vast oceans, there was much time for reflection. Standing on deck one evening with the breezes sweeping softly over the stern, Rullie gazed absentmindedly at the waveless horizon as he had done a hundred times, and longed for home. On many journeys he had met men who travelled the world searching for a spiritual home they seldom, if ever, found. He felt fortunate that the nearer he came to shores of England, the more he looked forward to seeing the familiar, the things he never failed to miss. To be able to read trees like country signposts and distinguish every songbird by its call. To hear again the sound of church bells and appreciate the sense of irony peculiar to his countrymen. Most of all, Rullie yearned for his wife's warmth and the fragrance of her skin.

In the second week of October, just before twilight as the swallows winged overhead, he turned into the driveway at Wexton Abbas. On opening the door of their cottage he saw Charlotte sitting at the piano, her beautiful hands reaching over the keys as she concentrated on a favourite piece by Chopin. The sight never failed to move him, feeling as he did that she played more gracefully each time he returned. Leaving off abruptly when she saw her husband, she walked quickly towards him. 'How wonderful to see you! You cannot know how pleased I am,' she said in a caressing voice, slipping her arms around his neck as they embraced.

Three of the four seedlings he had brought from Hunza perished. The fourth, however, turned into a healthy plant. It was placed in its own small clay pot containing only the finest of potting soils. Tiny roots were gently spread into the hole and the greatest care was taken when watering. The seedling's fragile stem would in time grow tall, with a vigorous sprouting of leaves. In order to shelter it from wind and frost, Rullie placed the pot under glass in a sunny corner of his walled garden, near an avenue of pleached hornbeams with arms linking like lovers.

Sir William received the rhododendron seeds at Kew with his usual enthusiasm. 'What a find, my dear fellow. Splendid, quite splendid.'

After travelling back from London, Rullie resumed his daily routine. At nine o'clock precisely each morning, he met with Gibbes who could often be spotted in his old tweed jacket wheeling a barrow about the beds or propagating new plants in the nursery. Together they walked round the constantly evolving arboretum to cast their eyes on any recent growth. Everywhere he went the russet tones of bronze and sorrel, the deep plums and purples of late autumn, embraced him. As they passed by an avenue of copper beeches, their cinnamon skirts sweeping the grass beneath them, Rullie turned to the gardener.

'Coming into this silent world is like entering a place of meditation, don't you agree?' he said, kicking the fallen leaves into the air with every step.

'Aye. I've always thought that a man's disposition has much to do with his involvement with nature,' Gibbes replied.

Both men were in agreement about many things.

If truth be told, Rullie secretly hoped his creation – a rich legacy of trees to bring people a sense of peace and wonder – would speak for him in perpetuity.

Encouraged by Charlotte, Rullie had adopted the habit of telling her tales of the mysterious worlds through which he had recently travelled, as a way of involving her in his work. Since she derived such obvious pleasure from listening to them, he developed the knack of infusing his stories with minute observations, seductive and piquant. Some would say he was prone to a slight exaggeration but this he would have dismissed as unthinkable. It was exactly how events appeared to him, no more and no less. He told his stories as though he were turning the pages of a book that might otherwise go unread.

'In the Punjab I was enjoying a quiet sherry on the verandah with an old retired colonel who suddenly insisted that his servant man haul down the Union Jack because it clashed with the sunset,' recalled Rullie as they sat together one evening. Charlotte was enchanted.

Her imagination ravenously absorbed his description of his brief stay in Zanzibar. She could almost taste the sea. She found herself standing in the labyrinth of narrow alleyways linking the whitewashed houses to the ancient harbour where, despite being outlawed, slaves were still sold. Where dhows from Persia arrived on the monsoon wind, their wooden holds filled with cargoes of silk and Chinese pottery. She watched as her husband climbed aboard a vessel owned by a local Sheikh of some standing.

'In the heat of the day I lay on carpets spread across the deck and accepted offerings of Turkish sweetmeats dusted in a powder of fine sugar,' mused Rullie looking into the far beyond, as if spinning a web out of nothing.

While he conversed with his host, she could clearly see the young Arab boy who fanned him with a large palm frond and for many hours sprinkled rose-water on his face and arms.

'How delightful,' she laughed.

During the long and lonely evenings when her husband was away and a child of her own seemed a distant dream, it was sometimes the anticipation of these stories that prevented Charlotte from occasionally lapsing into a state of melancholy.

It was natural that there would be one tree revered above all others by Rullie. On his travels he felt a certain affection for the comforting roundness of the mango tree, its ripe fruit dripping through dark leaves like fattened raindrops. He enjoyed the communal life shared with villagers who sat in its shade in the heat of the day. The pale eucalyptus was another favourite. Random washes of light and dark dissolving round its belly and the delicious smell of thin blue-grey leaves when crushed; bark sloughing off like an unwanted skin. He was fond of the giant baobabs which dotted the parched yellow grasses of the savannah like rooted elephants, serene in their solitude. Once, two thousand miles to the east of where Livingstone was busy crossing the dark continent, Rullie had picked up for a song a basket of seed-pods from the strange trees.

But it was the noble beech which he considered God's most perfect creation and which he entirely loved. The native broad-leaf possessed a natural, elegant dignity. Whenever he stood beneath one he felt in awe of the architectural beauty of its silver-green trunk rising effortlessly upwards into a mass of branches which slithered over each other like careless snakes before cascading downwards in a languid confusion of leaves. The whole shape a perfect symmetry. Whenever the need came upon him he would press his palms against the tree's smooth bark, as if the process of communication might reassure both man and plant that all was right between them.

While Rullie had been away, Jamie MacLellan had fallen in love with a tight-rope walker after bringing a circus to Wexton Abbas as a summer treat for the villagers. Once she and her troupe had moved on, his bruised heart wished to keep her memory alive, at the forefront of his numerous conquests – at least for the moment. He decided to erect a small fountain in the shape of a woman at one end of the village green. Strict instructions were given to the local stonemason to make it to scale with satisfactory proportions: 'She must have the legs of a dancer and the breasts of a goddess.'

A few of the older villagers thought it preposterous. Others, knowing full well that MacLellan was often the victim of his own impetuosity, merely smiled at his indulgence.

Life in the meantime held a soothing equilibrium for Rullie.

He and his wife lived frugally enough, having little need, except for a yearly trip together, for those frivolities and luxuries enjoyed by townspeople. Indeed, having managed his estate prudently, he was pleased to find that the small amount of money saved each year, after all arboretum expenses were paid, had now accumulated into a sum big enough to build a sizeable glasshouse. The abolition of a stiff tax on glass greatly influenced his decision. The building was to be situated along the west-facing side of the walled garden and here he would house colourful specimens from tropical rainforests – bamboos and palms, hibiscus and orchids would grace its interior. He would include frangipani, the delicate temple flower of Buddhists, whose subtle scent he knew would give Charlotte much pleasure.

The task of designing the structure was consigned to an architect recently arrived from Louisiana. Because of the unique construction of the dome – which was to resemble a giant pumpkin – some believed the building would be unstable. To be on the safe side, a model was first constructed. Extra hands eagerly signed up for the job and within weeks wooden scaffolding, iron bars and acres of glass could be found scattered all over the grass. To test its safety the architect, much to the workmen's chagrin, barked at them like a sergeant major: 'Now I want you to run back and forth together in time, then jump up and down to make sure it is safe.'

'What the devil does he think we are? A bunch of pudding-heads?'

As a final measure a few army troops stationed nearby were called in to march about. The model failed to collapse and the work went ahead. Curved iron struts, like the ribs of a huge whale, arrived daily. An order of five thousand small glass panes in a fish-scale design caused great excitement among the locals. When he wasn't supervising the building work, curbing the architect's excesses, and ensuring that the pulleys to open the huge sliding windows were suitably strong, nothing gave Rullie more pleasure than strolling arm in arm with Charlotte round the property or listening to her play after dinners given for their friends – local landowners and village notables. On fine evenings the windows of the drawing room were opened to catch the breeze before the cold set in, the scent of the last of the climbing roses resting lightly on the night air.

Although this was not strictly his line of business, Rullie was pleased the young apricot plant grew strong and thrived. Local fruit growers began to take a keen interest in the unusual little sapling and it wasn't long before Rullie and his brother began digesting the concept that such a plant might make a tidy profit for the estate. The village would also benefit.

Within a few weeks a decision was made by all, including Jamie MacLellan who had conveniently managed to overcome his initial fears and offered extra funding, that Rullie should return to Hunza to purchase more seedlings. After a proposed plant-collecting trip to China which had recently grudgingly granted access to a handful of foreigners, he would return by way of the small mountain kingdom.

Since the possible outcome of the venture was of the utmost importance and the itinerary circuitous, he packed his bags on the last day of March, 1857, not forgetting his flask of whisky and the small ammonite he kept as a talisman. In the early mist he walked to the waiting horse and carriage with Charlotte, held her tightly to him as though he would never let her go, kissed her goodbye, and set off once more for the tallest mountains in all the world

A steamboat carried him to the port of Alexandria. Fortunate to find suitable connections, he travelled a thousand miles over deserts and plains before crossing through the most northern part of Persia. A fortnight later he skirted the border of Afghanistan on horseback and traversed the frozen passes of the Parmir mountains until he arrived, nearly two months after his departure, in Xinjiang. Travelling at such a leisurely pace over many long weeks, the differing landscapes of the earth seem to change at a scarcely discernible rate. On days when Rullie was particularly tired, he noticed little difference in the endless, remote stretches between Bukhara and the foothills of Samarkand, a distance of over a hundred miles. To make things easier for himself once in Xinjiang, a place where strangers were seldom received with open arms, he simply cut his hair, donned the clothes of a Chinaman and set off. No one bothered him at all.

In the bazaar in Kashgar he was fortuitous in meeting a tea merchant from Canton who happened to have in his basket cuttings of a new species of weeping willow which grew in his garden. After exchanging money and polite bows Rullie proceeded to the next village where he managed to fulfil the request of a Dorset landowner who had offered him one hundred guineas to purchase a small bag of magnolia seeds. The Chinese trader assured him that in time every spring they would produce a thousand flowers of the palest pink, like the inside of a sea shell.

After completing his tasks Rullie turned south and, constantly checking his course with his compass, headed for the border. The journey was slow and he was delayed by days of mountain rain beating down like liquid steel into the confines of a cramped, dripping tent. On the third morning as he peered through the rain, soaked to the skin and hungry, he wondered if those higher up the plant chain – the curators, the nurserymen and collectors – had any real notion of the difficulties lowly paid plant hunters confronted in the dark, forbidding places of the world.

Lying on his thin blanket that night he was gripped by loneliness – months of prolonged isolation inevitably took a heavy toll. To comfort himself he conjured up the many creatures he had seen on his recent travels. He could see them clearly in his mind's eye – the shy gazelles, lone black bears, wild blue sheep and the lazy water buffaloes. He remembered the sleepy gharials in the river pools, monkeys and golden jackals bent on business, the occasional flick of a tiger's tail as it disappeared through the long grass; fields and forest floors crawling with beetles and grasshoppers, frogs and darting lizards. Skies filled with birds. He saw the snow pigeons and white-bellied herons, the noisy song babblers and the bright orange bills of the bulbul, the drifting kites and vultures picking at left-overs. He thought of the rare cranes, purple sunbirds, hornbills and the rushed flight of small green parakeets. He tried to remember them all.

Within a few days his mood had lightened considerably after he had successfully hunted down and dug up six small plants of a variegated bamboo much in demand by Kew. Two weeks later when Rullie eventually reached the end of the valley leading to the village of Zafran Khan, he knelt in the shade of a wind-twisted tree and drank from the icy waters of the tumbling river. Behind the town yawned the dark mouth of a narrow gorge hemmed in by a succession of precipices – immense, forbidding and still covered in snow. An eagle circled lazily in the sky above him. As he walked through a rough field bordering the terraces of mulberry and apricot trees, he heard the eerie, haunting cry of peacocks roaming the garden below Baltit Fort.

As Rullie reached the stream which fed Zafran Khan's orchards, he heard the burble of female laughter nearby. His curiosity roused, he tied his horse and mule to a tree and began walking slowly forward, following the dusty path until he came to a spot where the stream was flanked by a grove of poplars. Standing like sentinels, the trees offered almost complete privacy.

Almost.

A pale green garment and simple veil hung from one of the branches, like a peace offering left by the wind. As he peered through the fretwork of leaves, the afternoon sun drenching the water in golden light, he suddenly felt breathless.

For kneeling on the rocks by a shallow pool was the young girl, the one with the almond eyes. There was the barest murmur of wind on the surface of the water. As she cupped her hands to catch the drops, water being poured from an urn cascaded over her slender olive-brown body. He could not help but notice, since it was in his direct line of vision, the sinewy arch where the small of her back swept into a pronounced curve beneath the diaphanous sarong slung loosely round her hips.

She laughed as with deft movements her servant girl rubbed oil into her long black hair, brushing away tendrils from her uplifted face and softly, languidly, stroking her skin. They were almost entwined, like two dancers in an intimate, abstract ballet. Beside them, in a small cage, was a bird whose sweet notes rose on the late spring breeze.

It was an image of singular beauty and for a moment Rullie

was unable to tear his eyes away. He stood there for another few minutes before reluctantly averting his gaze and stealthily retracing his route, careful not to step on any leaves or twigs which might betray his position. He remounted his pony and continued his climb up the moraine.

As he neared the stone walls of the fortress, fragments of the scene he had just witnessed swirling in his mind, he happened to glance up. There on the windy terrace, his arms folded, stood Zafran Khan – looking down at him with penetrating eyes, the colour of cold steel.

'I have been waiting for your return, Englishman,' he said in a cool, dispassionate voice, as soon as Rullie entered the building. It was as if the ruler whose every whim was catered to had nothing better to do with his days than wait for an outsider to distract him. Having spent many months away from his own country far away on the other side of the world it was easy for Rullie to forget, before passing the long, clamorous queue at the gates, that business was not just a monopoly of towns and cities. Life in the most isolated villages possessed rituals, minute and exacting, crucial to their smooth running, with people scurrying to and fro like ants upon a mission.

'Come, sit down. Today I have many things to attend to before you tell me your reasons for returning ,' said the Mir.

Rullie sat down on a small hard stool, drinking scented tea from a shallow bowl offered to him by a servant, and watched men of the village arriving with letters and reams of documents – they scarcely glanced in his direction. A listless procession of villagers with complaints, eager to escape the perpetual wind, were ushered in and listened to. Curious children were ignored as they peered through an open window. Zafran Khan, behind whose reserve lay an obvious intelligence, greeted all comers in the same aloof manner.

Towards dusk the ruler completed the task of sending off his annual tribute of gold dust to the Chinese in Xinjiang – the small casket entrusted to a servant who left on horseback. The two hounds and two horses he also owed would be leaving at daybreak. The Mir invited his guest to join him in sitting cross-legged on the floor. For an hour they talked, occasionally eyeing each other with polite suspicion, but mostly content enough to be in the other's company. After a simple meal of beef, chapattis and ghee, Rullie was invited to stay. He was taken with little ceremony to a primitive mud-brick house, attached to the fortress. Grass and rushes were strewn on the earthen floor. A small fire had been lit, its smoke escaping listlessly through a square hole in the roof. Permission had been granted for him to pass through the kingdom but to linger no longer than necessary and this was to be his home for five days only. That night Rullie fell into a strange sleep, his dreams wandering over water, his thoughts caressing the impossible.

The following morning, while wandering through the village he chanced upon a man whose skin was not that of an Indian, pulling a cartful of bricks through the muddy street. Around his feet a few ducks waddled aimlessly. He appeared to have a timid nature, almost like a feral animal, his fortunes seemingly in decline.

'Sir, perhaps you can help me?' asked Rullie Montrose.

'Not now, I am busy.'

He was a Frenchman and it was plain he was a man desperate to be in a hurry. To be going somewhere, anywhere, to be doing something useful. The two men from the opposite side of the world walked together, one trying to shrug off the other as one would an insistent mongrel.

'Would you happen to know if a rare flowering plant grows hereabouts?'

The Frenchman stopped his wheeling and looked at the ground. It was a moment before he spoke.

'When I was ten years old, my parents were killed in a caravan raid. The people here took me in and have been good to me. I can say nothing.'

He went on his way before the Englishman could detain him any longer, his awkward movements filled with the dignity of the downtrodden. And Rullie wondered how it was that such an alluring place exuded such an intimidating disquiet.

As he continued walking around the village he found himself

still as much an object of curiosity as on his last visit. One by one villagers came out of their houses to gaze at his pale face and hair before giving him a shy smile. For a while he was surrounded by young children who pointed at his strange clothes and whispered and giggled to each other behind their hands. Deciding to explore further Rullie found a small path which he had not seen before, leading from the village up to Zafran Khan's fortress. After gently shaking off the children tugging playfully at his britches, he started up the narrow track which twisted and turned up an uneven slope before giving way to a flat circular outcrop. As he came to the top he saw standing in the middle of a meagre patch of grass – the young girl. And directly behind her stood the dark, imposing figure of her father, a fierce wind off the mountain whipping up the edges of his cloak.

They appeared to be in disagreement. While she kept her head bowed, nervously fingering the folds of her pale blue dress, the Mir was talking sharply to her. His voice was not raised but had the coldness of an angry man determined to remain calm in a delicate situation. At the sound of footsteps on the rocky path they both turned their heads in Rullie's direction. Interrupted in mid-sentence Zafran Khan abruptly ceased speaking. The young girl looked steadily at Rullie for the longest time and apart from the sound of the wind, all was silent around them. Then, unseen by her father behind her, she suddenly gave him a smile of such unexpected radiance that Rullie felt his heart lift.

'What interests you here, Englishman?' asked Zafran Khan eventually.

Rullie did not answer.

Zafran Khan sighed as he walked to his daughter's side.

'There is nothing for you on this mountain. Come child, it is time to return home.'

After lowering her eyes she turned to face her father and with her hand firmly gripped by his, the two of them walked back in the direction of the fortress.

Before they turned the corner the Mir glanced over his shoulder back to where Rullie was standing and said curtly, 'We will meet again tomorrow.'

As dawn broke on the second day, Rullie was summoned to the hall. Courtiers, talking in excited voices, fell silent and bowed low as the Mir arrived.

'Come. We are riding south,' he commanded as he adjusted his riding coat of thick animal fur around him and swept his long whip off a ledge.

Riding together, the two men set off down the valley, accompanied by a hundred men, their horses foaming at the bit. Banners fluttered in rhythmic waves from their flanks. Above them screeching kites dipped and soared in a bid to escape the noise of drummers and surnai pipers. The entourage crossed the turbulent river on a rickety bridge where the waters were less swollen and headed towards a field where horses and riders from the neighbouring village of Nagar waited. The air was filled with the nervous tension of men whose voices grew rowdier, wilder as they grew nearer.

'You will see how fine our horsemen are,' said Zafran Khan, turning to Rullie, the assurance in his voice clearly convinced that there could be none better.

'Mountain polo is a dangerous game. It has been our sport for many centuries. Perhaps you do not know that 'polo' is Baltit for ball.'

Under a larkspur sky players from the two sides, one led by the Mir, faced each other like miniature armies. A muffled roar echoed across the mountain slopes as they galloped up the field towards each other. Zafran Khan proved himself a man of splendid energy, wheeling and turning his horse as sticks clashed together, hanging from his mount at impossible angles to hit the ball as he and his men bore down on their opponents like men possessed. The spectacle was a mass of flesh in frenzied anarchy, stamina and pace beyond imagination, balls and mallets in flight, crowds fleeing in terror. Feckless riders drove their animals beyond their limits, ignoring with cruel deliberation each laceration, each cry of pain.

Rullie realised it hardly mattered to men who knew full well the upkeep of the ponies, which ate up a sizeable portion of a Mir's annual budget, was entirely his own affair. By the afternoon, two horses had dropped dead of heart failure and a number of players had suffered broken bones without complaint.

'My people believe that if you can ride like the winds of heaven, you will escape your enemies on earth,' said a victorious Zafran Khan. As if the day of danger and pain for him had produced nothing untoward.

But for Rullie the day had slipped by as a disturbing dream in which all was chaos and destruction, where riders, sky and horses were all one colour, the colour of blood. When the game was over and the sounds of the surnai pipers had faded away, the men departed for the village without delay. At the entrance to the fortress Zafran Khan bade Rullie a polite farewell and vanished into the gloom of his own world.

For the next two days, shadowed by a watchful servant, Rullie roamed the hillsides, the silent valleys and meadows above the glaciers, searching for a sign of the flowering plant's existence. He trampled over upland scrub beneath a row of rocky peaks which soared into the sky like the spires of a cathedral where it was said a local princess lay petrified in their midst. A small herd of wild yak with long dense fur sensed his presence from afar and he watched them flee across the barren slopes. He passed the shepherds' huts to which the men of Hunza came in summer with their flocks, and combed through the orchards, carefully, tier by tier, as if looking for clues in a murder mystery. Hours were spent criss-crossing the numerous stone channels which snaked across the slopes and carried water from the glaciers on which the fruit trees' existence depended. Rullie forced himself to continue searching for it was his nature to pursue the unattainable.

Despite his dogged persistence he could find nothing, absolutely nothing, that excited his curiosity. What few scrawny plants he found were too inferior to enumerate compared with the magical apparition he had built up in his mind. He only noticed that all around him were wonderfully coloured butterflies, turquoise, silvery-blue and green, which followed him everywhere as if he had about him an irresistible nectar that carried on the wind. Eventually, overcome by the weariness that follows disappointment, Rullie climbed the hill at dusk and returned to his small house. He dropped exhausted onto the rushes and for a while listened to the wind whistling outside, dispirited that the mystery of the remote mountain valley remained so utterly impenetrable.

A little after daybreak Zafran Khan sent a servant to invite him to celebrate their victory on the polo field that evening. As he waited for the appointed hour Rullie sat cross-legged beside his paltry fire. It wasn't long before it petered out, leaving his room in total darkness and forcing him outside to sit in the light of the rising moon. The night sky was clear and already dotted with stars. As he gazed at them he suddenly noticed a small movement in the distance. Four figures were making their way silently up the steep pathway towards his dwelling. When they arrived he saw they were women from the village, a large loose bundle carried on the back of the first. He could only make out the vague outline of their faces but sensed they were neither old nor young. Without much ado they ushered him back inside and made signs for him to take off his coat and trousers.

Giving in to their silent demands, he stood in the middle of the room unclothed and pliant, curious to see what happened next. One of the women proceeded to tie his hair back into a tight knot before pointing to the ground where he was to lie down. As soon as he closed his eyes he found a second woman kneeling beside him. With long skilful strokes she rubbed a musky balm all over his body, his arms, his legs. Her hands were soft and supple – not at all rough. The third woman kept gently running her fingers backwards and forwards through his hair. Her subtle touch on the back of his neck was caressing, soothing, and Rullie soon began to feel he was an experiment in a dream. At one point a beam of moonlight shone briefly through a chink in the doorway and out of the corner of his eye he glimpsed the fourth woman bending down in the dark to unfold the bundle. It consisted of a number of garments which she laid carefully down one by one on the floor. The women continued their work for over an hour and during the entire time they exchanged not a word.

When they had finished the first woman offered him her hand to pull him up. She untied his hair. She then invited him to step into a light pair of trousers which was tied firmly round his waist. Over that was placed a loose silk shirt and a heavy cloak of the softest weave with gold flecks in the wool which glittered in the darkened room. As they arranged the clothes the women patted and smoothed each layer, quietly murmuring as women do, to make sure the outfit fitted as neatly and tidily as possible. A heavy belt with silver amulets hanging off it was finally placed around Rullie's waist to keep everything in place. To complete the outfit a soft pair of emerald green leather shoes and a silk turban were left on the low rush bed. Once they had completed their task one by one the women clasped both his hands in each of theirs, bowed and silently left the small mud-brick house.

Rullie arrived at the Mir's home to find a sea of red and black banners hanging high on the roof of the fortress, which fluttered like whispers in the breeze. The whole garden, vaulted over by the skies and the stars, was illuminated by a thousand small brass lanterns. It seemed as though the whole of the village poured through the gates. Goats slaughtered for the occasion were placed on a large fire, its flames flicking upwards like wishes bound for heaven. Nearby a huddle of old crones whose stained teeth glinted in its glow banged on small wooden drums. Behind them several others were playing a strangely hypnotic tune on their surnai pipes. Younger women, in brightly coloured costumes and wearing modest strings of coral, silver and turquoise around their necks, exchanged sweet dishes with each other. Rullie thought he recognised two of them from a few hours before. He noticed small groups of old men with bowed backs and long beards dyed scarlet with henna, their cloth robes thickly studded with little white feathers for extra warmth. He heard them talking in low voices as they sipped wine stored in earthenware jars – Cordell had mentioned that the people of Hunza were very fond of drinking and dancing. Several of the men, squatting down around the fire to keep warm, had a bemused look in their eyes as they watched wisps of smoke from their long carved pipes curl into the air.

The Mir wore a magnificent brocade robe and a golden turban. His wives, equally opulently dressed, sat beside him on silken cushions spread under a large mulberry tree. Even ladies belonging to his harem were invited, their appearances enhanced by rouge and pomade. Not far from them Rullie stood in his newly acquired finery surrounded by a dozen fine-featured men wearing small woollen caps with upturned brims. Behind their bold eyes lay jovial expressions – as if they were delighted to include a stranger who knew nothing of their customs or language. As the women of the court milled around they smiled at him, regarding him as one does an exotic, curious object. Out of politeness he accepted a fiery liquid brewed from mulberries from one of them and found it burned his throat.

As his glance strayed into the shadows beyond the fire, he saw seated next to Zafran Khan four young women, one of whom wore a garment of purest white. Two others were laughing together and the fourth young woman was sitting as still as a prayer. On her wrist her small bird was singing as if its heart would burst. She was staring intently out of the dark at him as if, any minute, she would step through the flames to be by his side and in her eyes he read a hint of despair. Mesmerised by what he saw, he stood for a while, his eyes fixed upon hers. Suddenly oblivious to everything around him.

He barely registered the music changing into a beat that was throbbing, expectant. As the new moon sliced the sky over the mountains, he saw young village girls wearing bells on their ankles snake their way one by one into a circle and begin swaying to the rhythms of the night. Shyly, then with growing confidence, they tucked their veils discreetly behind their lustrous black hair, allowing them to free their arms. With subtle, graceful movements they danced for the Mir and their men. The firelight cast an amber glow on their skin and Rullie,

74

almost like a neutral observer, was only vaguely aware of the sensual undulation of hips and delicate wrists fluttering like tiny golden birds. As ancient rhythms were beaten out on the drums the dancing became more impassioned, provoking the dancers into a trance, the swirl of their feet sending dust billowing into the night.

In the hours that followed, he saw in the dimness behind the sea of colour, that her eyes seldom left his own. Wanting nothing more than to be near her, Rullie walked instead to the end of the garden which jutted out over the valley, into a corner where darkness favoured the imagination and where he hoped the beating of his heart might be stilled. Before he could unravel his thoughts he noticed the tallest flowers at his feet were outlined in the subtle glow of a lantern. The faintest sensation of a flower he could not name wafted over the night air.

She was there. Beside him, as if she had been so all his life.

As he inhaled the sweet fragrance of her breath, she raised herself on her toes and briefly brushed her lips against his cheek. Her mouth was softer than silk. When a slight breeze ruffled her little bird's feathers, causing it to flutter out of fright onto his shoulder, he saw the young girl's eyes shining with a burning urgency. She opened her palms towards him in a small gesture of hopelessness and he held them tight, as if that way she might leave an imprint of herself upon him.

Looking into her bewitching face, he felt a wistful longing for what could never be. He had nothing to give her but it took nothing to reach into his breast pocket and draw out his cherished ammonite, timeless, perfect, its iridescent, silvery-green shell shining in the moonlight. For more years than he could remember it had been his inseparable talisman. He pressed the curved fossil into her hands and folded her fingers slowly over it. Within seconds she had vanished, fading like an illusion back to the protective wing of her family.

That night Rullie found the lightest of feathers on the sleeve of his coat.

He plucked if off and rolled it over and over, like a minute wave, around his finger.

Then pressed it close to his heart.

On his final morning Rullie packed his bags, carefully removing twelve gold chips before closing the straps, and went into the fortress to pay his respects to Zafran Khan. Without a murmur he was escorted by his host down into the bowels of the building where, in a cave of silence, a locked iron door was clanked open by a guard. Rullie stepped inside and was greeted by an extraordinary sight, a world so far removed from reality that he hardly knew where first to feast his eyes. Spoils from years of plunder littered the dank room, a setting that only enhanced their surreal quality. A mound of gold and silver reached the ceiling, antique suits of chain armour, a Parisian music box, bottles of quicksilver, precious jewels exploding with colour, guns, powder, bullets fashioned out of garnet. In one corner beneath a cloth of woven gold lay a mountain of apricot stones enclosing seeds from the Mir's prized trees.

Zafran Khan, appeared to be enjoying himself. The look of astonishment on the Englishman's face was obviously the subject of much satisfaction. As he looked around the room he stared for a moment at the few stones which lay scattered beside the mound.

'Ah, my friend, you seem impressed. All you see here are things I took from others. Everything is mine now. Only one small sack of seeds I am prepared to sell you. That is all.'

He seemed reasonably pleased with the amount of gold that Rullie, in a daze, proffered. The Mir then bent down and snatched up one of the stones. He caressed it fondly, studying the deep, pitted grooves in the shell and said as though rehearsing the lines of a well-worn monologue: 'My daughters are as precious to me as these seeds. The eldest I must look after, for she has recently been widowed. The middle two are married to fine men from the valley.'

He looked steadily into the eyes of the man standing opposite him and continued without a trace of alteration in his voice: 'My youngest daughter is betrothed. To a distant cousin from the eastern lands of Afghanistan. She will marry within the year.'

He put his hands together, gave a slight nod of dismissal and said: 'Now it is time for you to leave.'

Rullie, for no reason other than a sudden sense of disbelief, found his heart had crystallised into a small, tight knot.

He collected his belongings and left for England within the hour, passing near the glade where he had once encountered the old hermit. He glimpsed him there, sitting on a log playing his pipe as he watched bee-eaters skim through the leafy depths of the forest.

Once he was through the woods Rullie looked back over his shoulder.

Only once.

Standing alone on the windy terrace far above him he saw the young girl. She was calling out to him as if begging him to come back, a flimsy piece of white silk waving crazily, like a desolate love letter, from her outstretched hand.

News had reached Rullie earlier that momentous events were unfolding in the country through which he travelled. It seemed the British had not been totally successful in paring the claws of Oriental tigers who knew that they could not be held in submission forever. An Irish plant hunter he had recently bumped into on a mountain pass told him the spark that fired the recent rebellion of sepoys near Delhi in May had been fuelled by rumours that rifles used cartridges greased with beef and pork tallow. As cows were sacred to Hindus and pork obscene to Muslims, biting off the ends of the cartridges when loading was an action guaranteed to alienate both, and soldiers of each faith simply refused to obey. Landlords, peasants and Bahadur Shah, the last Moghul emperor and by now a feeble old man, rose up with the sepoys – the maharajahs largely remaining loyal to the British. Delhi was taken, the mutiny spread like a bush fire and at Cawnpore six hundred officers, women and children were slaughtered. Shot, bayoneted or hacked to death by sabres – their bodies were flung down a well. The beginning of India's long struggle for freedom was underway.

Needing to escape the dangerous debris of combat directly to the south, Rullie took an alternative route. While fierce fighting continued, he left India on horseback by hugging the contours of its border with Afghanistan until he reached the ocean. Eight hundred miles away he could be found on the River Euphrates, having sailed into the calm waters from the Gulf of

Persia. Three weeks later when he arrived by boat from Turkey onto the shores of home, tales of the Indian Mutiny and its horrors were on the lips of everyone.

In late September, at twilight, the carriage carrying Rullie turned into the driveway at Wexton Abbas. On hearing the crunch of wheels and the snorting of tired horses Charlotte came running out of the cottage to meet him, her thick hair streaming out behind her like musical notes on the wind.

'Thank God you're safe,' she said, her eyes glistening with pleasure.

She smiled as he kissed her and gave her a dark green sari made of the finest silk such as high-caste Hindu women wore on the other side of the world.

After dinner Rullie led Charlotte upstairs to their bedroom and with the urgency of a man who has been away many months, made love to her with a fevered intensity. Time and time again for hours. Afterwards, Charlotte lay awake in the dark, her hearing focused on her husband's still, shallow breathing and wondered why she felt a vague unease, a dull ache in the pit of her stomach.

It was brief. It only lasted a second.

'You are my world,' she whispered, her face next to his on the pillow.

Later, as he drifted off to sleep, his head resting on her breast, she heard her husband say in a barely audible whisper, 'We will always be safe, here together.'

But however hard Charlotte tried to still her mind in the remaining hours of the night, she found the margins between sleep and wakefulness were indiscernible.

Kew viewed the new species of willow brought back with keen interest and suitably rewarded their plant hunter, while the Dorset landowner was so overcome by the magnitude of his magnolia seeds that he forgot himself entirely and engulfed Rullie in a suffocating bear-hug . At home great care was taken with the new batch of apricot stones which were first soaked in water for a day to soften their outer shell. They were then placed in moist peat moss in small glass jars and taken down to the cool, damp cellar. Within one hundred days the seeds had ripened and were ready to be placed into little clay pots in the glasshouse where they were as fussed over and protected as any newborn.

After six months away Rullie was intrigued by the changes in the tapestry of his burgeoning arboretum. While to others the growth of his trees might seem infinitesimal, his eyes only noticed wider girths, heavier branches, more abundant foliage – his children on the brink of adolescence. How transient was the beauty of a flower in comparison! How he looked forward to this time of year, especially to his Japanese maples, propagated from cuttings he had brought from China – in the days before Japan was opened up to foreigners. The small exotics were busily preparing for their autumnal dance, the splendour of their scarlet and butter-yellow finery only dimmed by the last of the evening light. Over the past few years calamities often greeted his return – trees stricken by pernicious blight, squirrels nibbling acorns or destroying dozens of young beech trees.

Rullie always felt a good deal of responsibility and anxiety in looking after his trees, in particular the older ones whose beauty, in his eyes, only grew more pronounced with age.

By now the glasshouse embraced numerous varieties of exotic plants, heated throughout the winter months by furnaces. And having been moved from its confines into a corner of the walled garden, the apricot sapling sat easily in its rural setting. It was now nearly two years old. Although it would be some years before it flowered, its shape and height were pleasing. Gibbes had been exemplary in his care. The soil around the plant was kept clear of weeds and grass so that ample moisture could reach the roots. The sun warmed its turning leaves and cast a small shadow onto the grass.

'Did you find anything truly unusual, exotic, this time in the tallest mountains in all the world?' asked Gibbes on his second morning home.

Rullie, standing in a pool of dappled light which filtered through the trees, was silent for a moment.

'Nothing more beautiful than what we have here.'

For a while after his return Rullie's life continued quietly and methodically. He was considerate of his wife's need for affection. He kept his own counsel and buried any uninvited thoughts in physical work. It was only in his second month home that it occurred to him he had not seen Jamie MacLellan since his return, having somehow forgotten their weekly rendez-vous at the Friar's Tuck.

It was a Tuesday. He waited until nightfall as Tuesday after-noons at the Scotsman's house were sacrosanct. He was an avid poker player and, joined by three of his more prosperous neighbours, it was an unbroken rule that play continue un-interrupted from two until six in the evening. Instead of chips, small pink cowrie shells found in an old smugglers' cove in Cornwall were used. Betting was high and rumour had it that fifty guineas regularly passed to the winner. Those in the vicinity were fully aware if luck had favoured MacLellan – snatches from *Don Giovanni* echoed across the lawn like the braying of a mournful donkey.

Rullie found him slumped in his chair, sipping a strong whisky. He had lost. Again. His gloom partially lifted on seeing his friend who, he noticed, was markedly thinner and somewhat dishevelled.

'MacLellan, I need your advice.'

The poker player shuffled a pack of cards absentmindedly, as if contemplating the intricacies of a winning hand just out of reach.

'Women problems, is it?'

'Of a sort.'

MacLellan was not to be put off by the vagueness of his answer.

'There can be little other when a man loses his appetite, changes his habits and adopts a preoccupied air.'

Pause.

'Is that so?'

It could be said that many Englishmen are apt to display an acute discomfit in disclosing what is in their hearts, to confide in another their most private concerns. And thus their inner life often remains largely impenetrable. Not unexpectedly, Rullie was brief,

'My wife seems unable to conceive. We both long for a child and the situation causes a certain degree of tension. Any suggestions?'

MacLellan picked up a three of spades which had fallen on the floor.

'A woman's world is unfathomable. Doctors are useless. Only another woman, wise in the ways of her own gender, could tell you what to do. You don't need me to tell you where to go.'

MacLellan was always bracingly realistic in his analysis of others' problems.

The next week found Rullie on the road to Lulworth where Allegra lived. He had told his wife that he was going to deliver some important seeds and would be back later that evening.

The sea mist was rolling in as he walked through the field that led to a wooden caravan, elaborately carved and garishly painted, decadently, as though for a carnival. It beckoned in the watery light like an irresistible beacon. A short distance away, tall limestone cliffs fell steeply away to an almost circular sandy cove far below. Behind the caravan, rolling hills curved into each other and offered their reassuring solidity to the skies. As he neared the caravan he looked up and saw a mass of sparrows drifting past like a floating net. Rullie climbed the steps up to the blue and yellow door and called out her name.

A smile lit up Allegra's face as she opened the door. She took him by the hand and seated him on the only chair by the stove. She wore a long black flowing robe, the opening of which was not fastened. Embroidered scarlet flowers matched the livid colour on her full, sensual mouth. Through the thin silk Rullie could see the swell of her breasts. There was around her, as usual, the heady scent of musk.

'What calamity brings you to me this time?' Allegra laughed, a flirtatious smile in her hazel coloured eyes.

'I have a dilemma. I needed someone to talk to .'

'Ah, with a little introspection most things can be solved.'

87

A small candle was brought to the small table and lit. Only one. Allegra was poor and candles cost too much to burn.

In her youth Allegra had been a temptress and even now her charms were not without their admirers. With raven hair swirling like smoke and the possessor of a splendid bosom, she proffered solace and encouragement in equal measure to those who asked. She could be pithy to the point of brusqueness, sometimes drank too much and lived in some disarray with her small dog, a spaniel, but there was about her an air of innocence. Twenty years previously Rullie was one of many men, including Jamie MacLellan, who had succumbed to her witchery and rapidly found himself in a condition not far from love. But she had moved on in her nomadic, gypsy existence and it had been a number of months before Rullie ceased to sigh for his youthful passion. In the intervening years the two had played in that intoxicating area between the possible and the destructive, but had fallen instead into a lasting friendship.

While they shared a bottle of wine he had brought, Rullie told her of his life since they last met. Of his work and travels, the trials of plant-hunting, but mostly of how fatherhood was proving elusive. Although he never alluded to it, Allegra soon understood, as women do, the tangled web of his heart. When he had finished speaking she leaned over and put her hands on his shoulders. He felt the attraction still there, quiescent, unspoken.

'Change your stars, Rullie Montrose. Cherish what is yours and you will lead a happier life.'

When he left she was sleeping, her little dog whimpering in its dreams at the foot of her iron bed.

A few days later, before the cold set in, Rullie decided to take his wife on a short trip which he hoped she might enjoy. They travelled first to London where they visited various museums and galleries. They took in a popular concert and enjoyed sitting in fashionable tea rooms, watching the animated bustle of the crowd. After three days they continued on their way to Deauville. For a week they stayed in a small hotel on the edge of the town which had seen better times. The couple spent their time immersed in one another and watched the ebb and flow of the sea echo their days. When the wind was not too strong they collected seashells, marvelling at their intricacy, and each evening they smiled at the culinary excesses of the French. One night an elderly gentleman from Cherbourg was seated at a table next to them. He invited them to accompany him the following evening to a play by Molière which was being staged in the grounds of a nearby chateau owned by an acquaintance. He mentioned with a smile that the wife of this man was particularly agreeable.

Madame Vaucamp had been once been an actress. Of little reknown. Some said she owned a brothel before her marriage. Others that she was still partial to entertaining a number of men. She possessed a waist so naturally small it seemed an impossibility. Golden hair fell in studied confusion down her back and from afar she looked like an ingénue fresh from the Parisian stage. It was only on closer observation that Rullie saw that her blithe insouciance masked an ancient, raddled beauty. Using every resource to keep reality at bay, she was entirely her own invention.

Monsieur Vaucamp, tall and silver-haired with the face of a hawk, was some years her junior. He had spent the past eleven years travelling, returning for one day only each year to see his wife on the day of her fête.

'What is the business that keeps you away so long?' asked Rullie of his host, as they walked to their seats.

'I deal in human commodities,' he laughed, with the air of one who never doubts his is a moral vocation. He was a slave-trader who bought for nothing young girls and boys in the ports of Mozambique and Zanzibar and shipped them to the Levant. To him life was money. Pure and simple. The ease with which young lives were ruined never entered his mind.

'Once my wealth permitted, I bought this chateau and had Madame Vaucamp fill it with fine antiques,' he boasted to Charlotte. Although they would never have said so, those who greedily accepted his wife's numerous invitations viewed her taste as lamentable.

With the cold night air seeping through their clothes, Rullie and his wife took scant pleasure in both the long complex play of which they understood little and the disturbing glimpse of a darker, more sinister world of collecting. When they finally returned to their room, they heaved a sigh of relief and returned to matters which comfort the senses, their affection falling upon them as softly and serenely as petals.

The sea voyage back to England was uncomfortably choppy. For the first two days after their return the wind gathered pace and clusters of dark, low clouds scudded across Wexton Abbas. On the third evening a huge storm raged, chaotic and unshackled. In the silence of their bedroom Rullie listened to the sound of the wind shrieking outside like an enraged virago – the soughing and cracking of heavy branches seemed never to end. At first light his feelings of dread mounted as he opened his front door and made his way to the arboretum. By now the storm had vanished. It was as if it had never been and in its place was an eerie silence. All over the garden trees had been ripped out of the ground and Rullie ran, shouting and stumbling over a sea of broken branches.

Gibbes and the other gardeners were already about, tearing at the debris, their anguish at seeing the devastation clearly palpable. It was as if someone had thrown a giant axe into the firmament. A tall Douglas fir and Scots pine, cut down in their youth, had fallen over each other like casualties of war. Gone were many of the Japanese maples, the tallest magnolia and the handsome dogwood. Mature deciduous trees – oak and chestnut, lime and elm – all had limbs maimed and torn. Where once precision and order had formed an arboreal cathedral, there was now a tangled mass of ruins. To Rullie, who dearly loved his trees, their loss felt like a bereavement.

He noticed the storm had been careful not to exclude the end of the glasshouse which housed the apricot seeds. Broken panes of glass were strewn everywhere. Although many of the plants inside were still standing, the seeds from Hunza had vanished without trace. But, as if celebrating the small miracle of its own survival, the little apricot tree, sheltered from the fiercest winds, stood unbowed and defiant. Overwhelmed by what the night had bought, Rullie walked in a daze over to the edge of the lawn. Through the mist which cast a ghostly silvery sheen over the park he saw that four of his beloved beeches had suffered a fatal blow, their shallow sensitive roots cruelly torn from under them. Rullie stood amid his shattered trees, his head in his hands as he considered what seemed like his own destruction.

Within three weeks, with the help of many men from the village, the worst of the debris in the arboretum was removed. The damage was marginally less than at first thought, but Rullie knew in his heart it would take years to get it back to anywhere near its best again. A fair number of hardy trees remained, however, and out of a sense of gratitude for their steady loyalty Rullie put his arms round two of the oldest and gave them each a heartfelt hug. The earth was once again raked and prepared and seed was sown. Hundreds of new glass panes were cut. Calder offered not one sou to help, explaining that any restoration was beyond the trust's means, but Rullie refused to delay matters further. As if to lay the ghosts of his fallen children to rest, he ordered what small trees and shrubs he could afford to be planted before the autumn completed its long, unhurried slide into winter.

At the beginning of January, MacLellan met with the village notables of Wexton Abbas to decide how they could best help Rullie restore the fractured beauty of his arboretum that spring. The Scotsman also had an interest in procuring, by fair means or foul it must be said, more apricot seeds. For the future of the village, naturally. The unwavering vision of the flowering plant also remained firmly in his mind, his curiosity as to its existence having lately got the better of him. Secretly, he thought it would make him a happy man to be amongst the first to have a glimpse of it.

'The doors of Hunza won't be open to Rullie Montrose

indefinitely,' he said, in a spirited attempt to whip up support.

Many of the villagers said it was lunacy. He was pushing his luck. Besides, since they might all be dead before they saw any profit from the production of apricots, it was impractical and expensive. The meeting ended in disagreement and it was left to MacLellan to inform Rullie that no further monies for future trips to Hunza would be forthcoming.

He knocked on Rullie's door later that afternoon. The two men withdrew into the study and MacLellan explained the outcome of the meeting. His friend looked steadily at him.

'I have never asked for any help from anyone.'

Silence.

'I'd gladly put up the money myself, but I'm a bit strapped for cash. For some confounded reason the merchant navy is cutting back on my timber,' said the Scotsman. Rullie stared at the patterns on the carpet as if in that way he might recognise the threads of his future.

He then turned and looked at MacLellan.

'I have a job to do. Besides it's essential I find more plants and cuttings for here.' He looked past his friend and said, 'I have no choice. Whatever the outcome I've decided to include Hunza in my travels.'

This came as little surprise to MacLellan who continued half-heartedly, 'How can you possibly consider the hardships and difficulties you will once again encounter? Not to mention the cost.'

Rullie quickly interjected, 'I sold a small painting left to me long ago by my father last month. I will use that money. No need to worry.'

'God in heaven, man, shouldn't you just drop the whole caboodle?' MacLellan said, momentarily forgetting his business acumen. He knew full well what parting with one of his father's few treasured possessions would have cost his friend. But alas, temptation would always be a heavenly demon. 'I always worry about you, my friend, until the day you return.'

He then picked up his hat and said good-night.

In March of 1858 Rullie turned thirty-six. News came from India that although peace had yet to be declared throughout the country, British forces had lifted the siege of Lucknow, ending the Mutiny. Having exacted their revenge on many of the rebels with a spate of hangings and executions, the British were beginning to mull over the far-reaching effects of the fighting, no doubt seeing it as a useful lesson on how to handle native troops. The East India Company was duly abolished and the British government assumed the administration of the Indian Empire. In the aftermath of the Mutiny, Queen Victoria stressed to all, 'There should be no hatred to a brown skin.'

By the end of the month Rullie's preparations for his expedition were completed. In the days leading up to his departure, Charlotte woke each morning from a repetitive dream in which she stepped one foot slowly in front of the other until she had reached the shadow of a guillotine. Although normally a woman of measured temperament, the vision unnerved her. She then did something she had vowed never to do. On their last day together, for the first time in all the years of their marriage, she begged him not to go.

'Something is not right. I know it.'

Rullie held her tightly to him. 'I must go.'

He felt a silent tear slide slowly down the side of his neck.

'I must.'

Early the next morning Rullie travelled to Paris where he boarded a train which would carry him south across Europe. The soothing sense of freedom granted on long train journeys eased his painful goodbye and as the green fields skimmed past, he began to feel a gradual release from everyday intrusions.

By a stroke of luck he chanced into conversation with a fellow traveller in his carriage. Robert Fortune, a gruff Scot, was a former Curator of the Chelsea Physic Garden. He was also a famous plant hunter, proficient in Mandarin and prone to disguising himself by wearing local dress. To pass the time as they travelled together Fortune recalled some of his clandestine adventures in China.

'A few years ago I began to shave my head and adopt a pigtail. I felt I looked rather fetching.' Fortune smiled at the memory. 'I managed to enter the forbidden city of Souchow unchallenged and was fortunate enough to find my double yellow rose there. Perhaps you have heard of it?'

It was common knowledge that, being the first plant hunter to bring back a wide selection of Chinese and Japanese plants, Fortune had ignited the Victorian passion for diverse and beautiful Oriental flora – jasmine, false larch, Chinese plum yew, umbrella pine among them.

'My greatest adventure of all though was smuggling twenty thousand Chinese tea plants and seedlings in my Wardian cases to the Indian Himalayas – to establish their tea industry, you understand.'

'And for that all Europe is in your debt. I salute your success,' Rullie replied, before the two men disembarked, shook hands and went their own ways.

Exactly five weeks after setting out from England, Rullie was immersed in the colourful chaos of Bombay harbour. There he purchased a mare and set off in a northerly direction. In front of him lay nearly a thousand miles. Whenever possible, night found him in one of the bungalows placed at lengthy intervals along the road where travellers and officials were welcomed.

He rose each day at dawn and rode until exhausted by the burning sun before crossing over the deserted regions of Rajputana and into the foothills of the Himalayas. One day on a narrow path he found himself joined by an Indian mail-runner, a *hikara*, his light sinuous body attuned to the high mountain air. Rullie knew little stopped these dedicated tribal men from getting their mail bags through to their destination. The runner spoke a little English and said in a sing-song voice as he jogged along, his head nodding from side to side, 'My main obstacle of course is being eaten by a tiger, but my greatest fears are trees possessing evil spirits. I will detour round these for many miles. Now I must run on. Good-day, sir.'

All was quiet on Rullie's travels to the tallest mountains in all the world. He saw no riots, no skirmishes, only villages with friendly inhabitants in valleys wild and silent where the wind on the mountains made a sound like the sea on the shore. He passed a wayside shrine on the road along which Buddhism once made its way to China. In a nearby lamasery he paid a small amount of gold for potted seedlings of a fragrant tree paeony cultivated in the garden. As he crossed the Hunza River, swollen by the melting snows, he glanced upwards and saw the fortress sitting in brooding isolation on the mountain ridge. Quickening his pace, he hoped that his arrival would not be met with suspicion.

On reaching the village Rullie heard the hushed voices of the inhabitants hum in the air around him. He noticed they were going about their day in a leisurely, rudderless way as if there was no particular need to push their lives forward. He sat motionless on his horse for a while and looked upwards beyond the apricot trees feathered with dying blossom. He searched the numerous small windows of the ancient edifice. All appeared shut, as inert as an old bird's nest, and he knew immediately that the young girl and her family had gone. Tearing his eyes away, he dismounted and led his animal up a path to the furthest end of the village, searching for a sign that seemed invisible.

For a moment Rullie felt his dreams had collapsed into dust. His last chance to find the beautiful flowering plant had been snatched from him and he would now never deliver to Kew this rarest of specimens, nor any extra apricot seeds to Wexton Abbas. And the young girl, the young girl had disappeared like a mirage from his life. He tried in vain to banish the flood of images swirling in his mind and barely heard the scuffling footsteps close behind him. Glancing over his shoulder he saw it was the old Frenchman he had met on his previous visit. There was no sign of his cartload of bricks but after a while the man with the timid nature plucked up the courage to speak:

'Your timing is bad, Englishman. Zafran Khan has taken his family and his hunting falcons across the border to Afghanistan to prepare for his daughter's marriage. Before the summer heat is upon us.'

He spoke in his native French.

Rullie could say nothing. He steadied himself by holding tightly onto the reins of his horse. He knew two options were open to him and that he would choose the only one that mattered. It was as though some unconquerable force had taken control of his heart, his mind, rendering him helpless. He took out his purse and poured a coin into the palm of his hand.

'I will give you one gold chip if you show me the quickest way to the border,' he said to the Frenchman.

At first the man seemed reluctant. He hesitated before replying.

'Two.'

A bargain was struck and the two men left together. From time to time the Frenchman turned round to ensure his companion was following him through the forests of poplar and birch trees down into the valley. Snow glistened on the distant peaks of the mountains far above them. The echo of hooves scraping over stones and squelching into the loose, sodden earth by a stream seemed to give the older man a simple pleasure. He was a man who possessed an altogether otherworldly approach to the immediate and, once again needed, it was if the burden of his days had fallen from his shoulders. As he walked in his fast shuffling gait, he sang the French songs of his childhood as though he had not a care in the world.

For ten days and ten nights they travelled west. Rullie felt as vulnerable as a blind man entrusting his every step into the hands of this odd companion. Whenever the Frenchman became tired he climbed up onto the horse behind the plant hunter, his legs swinging freely as he rode.

He said little and Rullie found it peaceful to be in his company.

In the remote Chitral valley they were careful to avoid the slow-moving caravans whose feudal travellers, flinty and temperamental, ran a successful business in slaves – often their own people. But their luck ran out early one morning. As they were climbing steadily up a mountain track, Rullie holding his horse's reins as he walked, they were suddenly overtaken by bandits brandishing long knives, who came out of nowhere. Unwittingly drawn into the skirmish, the Frenchman received a painful gash to his cheek. Mindful of the recent murder of two plant hunters Rullie rushed to his side and fired two shots from his pistol in their direction. Both flew harmlessly over the intruders' heads.

'Damn,' he shouted, realising that one of them, before fleeing, had fatally wounded his horse. The animal had served him well and he felt his loss keenly as they heaved its body down the rocky slope into the ravine, to be eaten by vultures. The two men had little choice but to continue on foot until they reached the Khyber Pass. There they shook hands and the Frenchman received the gold chips due to him.

'Au revoir, it has been a pleasure to travel with you,' was all he said.

Then both turned their back on the other to step over into their separate worlds. Rullie purchased a rackety old mule from a passing caravan and rode alone through the narrow, steep-sided pass that for many centuries had divided and linked empires and peoples; through which kings and warriors had passed; where Buddhist pilgrims and soldiers of fortune still trod a romantic, often perilous path.

The road stretched away towards the horizon until it was just a pale blue ribbon fluttering between the earth and sky. A carpet of fine sand, the colour of burnt almond, covered the ground over which Rullie travelled; the wind was still and the sun beat down on a land without life. Twilight laid a cloth of burnished gold over the towering hillsides of the Hindu Kush. There were times when he knew he might be risking death and should turn back. But by now all logic had evaporated under the weight of his feverish obsession. Two days into his journey he stopped at a small village beside a field of pale mauve opium poppies where friendly Pashtun tribesmen invited him to stay. The evening was cold and the villagers were warming themselves around the fire. Rullie slept under the stars on a blanket near the simple mosque, far away from the Muslim women inside the mud-brick walls of the compound.

In the black of night he was awakened by a pain so piercing, so terrible, he felt he had been stabbed. He leapt to his feet. No one was about. He looked for a snake but instead found a large scorpion crawling stealthily into the shadows beside the dying embers. Within moments a river of molten lava had invaded him. It raged through the veins and muscles of his arm and he felt the precise moment that the poison seeped into and captured each joint of his stricken limb. After drinking the remains of his whisky to ease his suffering, Rullie collapsed on the ground and surrendered to the rhythmic waves of pain throbbing through his body. Feverish, sweating, he moaned for many hours as he drifted in and out of the fiery abyss. Of all the acute suffering in his life, bouts of malaria, surgeons' scalpels, broken bones, nothing compared to this agonising realm into which he had innocently entered.

Before dawn the villagers found him dizzy and exhausted. Always vigilant of this most deadly of scorpions though knowing little could be done, they sent a young boy to sit beside him and press a cloth with water cold from the river onto his arm. He was small and nervous and had eyes the colour of topaz.

'Thank you, my young Afghan friend,' murmured Rullie as for endless hours the boy soothed his forehead and his burning arm.

There he stayed for the rest of the day until he began to slowly recover.

With the rising of the sun Rullie continued his journey until he saw, faint like camels on the desert's edge, the outline of Jalalabad. Step after weary step and still unwell, he eventually reached the outskirts of the town. There he found the husk of a dwelling that promised relief and he crouched in its welcome shade, his face brown and chafed with windburn. He was wearing clothing bartered from men at the previous village and as it was not unusual to see people of that land with blue eyes and sandy hair, he was left alone. It was as if he was invisible. He wandered slowly, deliberately, in the narrow streets of the bazaar among gleaming brass pots and dusty carpets woven in a hundred different colours. Amid a place of fragrance and filth, spices and cow dung, he searched for signs of an entourage recently arrived.

Then something he could hardly have imagined suddenly occurred. As he was fingering the soft materials of silk and cotton hanging outside a stall somebody inadvertently brushed against him. He looked round and recognised a tall rugged individual.

'Rullie Montrose, what on earth are you doing here?' Cordell asked incredulously.

'I have come to find Zafran Khan and his family.'

'What could you possibly want with them?'

Rullie averted his eyes and said in a steady voice: 'Do you know where they are staying?'

'It could only be at the summer court of the Emir, Dost

Mohammed. He is there with a few of his fifty-seven sons,' he laughed.

They walked together through a maze of alleyways lined with open sewers. At the far end of a street, crowded with veiled women and men with the most handsome of features, sat a large brick building hidden behind a screen of fraying eucalyptus trees. In the courtyard water from a small fountain of white marble and pale green mosaic rose up and sparkled against the sky. A number of turbaned Afghans with curved daggers slung round their hips milled aimlessly about. In one corner camels that had travelled from faraway lands lowered their legs to kneel in the dust.

'I will leave you here,' said Cordell. 'You'll need a bed tonight. I will find you. Be careful. Remember, this court, though cultured, can also be heartless.' He turned on his heels and soon disappeared into the bustling throng.

Rullie waited in the cool shade of the trees until eventually he saw the heavy doors of the building scrape open. Into the courtyard stepped a phalanx of veiled, chattering women. In their midst he saw a young girl. With almond-shaped eyes and loose hair reaching below the small of her back. Perched on her left wrist was a little bird. Gliding silently over the tiled courtyard, she was helped into a primitive type of palanquin. At one end she sat hidden from onlookers and the burning sun by two flimsy curtains of the lightest yellow silk. Four young men standing at each corner soundlessly lifted up the poles of the rickety wooden structure.

As the palanquin swung creakily from side to side coming through the gates, Rullie felt hypnotised by the faint tinkle of a single silver bell. Nearer, nearer to the trees until he thought the loud thumping in his breast could be heard. When it reached a spot exactly in front of where he was standing, the corner of a curtain was drawn back slightly.

The young girl looked straight into the eyes of Rullie Montrose.

She held his gaze for the longest moment.

She then let go of the curtain.

The silk folded over her and she moved away in a soft symphony of colour.

Despite the fact that Cordell managed to produce mutton and whisky out of thin air that evening, Rullie had little appetite for eating. He was in a reflective mood and when his host lightly touched upon the subject, his answer as to why he was in Jalalabad was not wholly plausible.

'Perhaps this part of the world has bitten too sharply into my soul.'

Cordell nodded, trying his best to understand, and continued with his dinner.

For his part, Rullie deduced Cordell was still constant in his cause and vulnerable to intrigues – busy playing cat and mouse with the Russians across the vast lands of the Hindu Kush and Pamirs.

Understandably in acquaintances thrown together un-expectedly, most of their evening was spent cautiously evading probing questions. They spoke of everything except that which mattered most to each of them. After a while Cordell showed his guest to his sparsely furnished room. It had a ceiling fan and large windows open to the hot, windless night. After closing the door, Rullie removed his clothes and lay beneath the thin cotton sheet. For what seemed like hours sleep was impossible.

At first he thought it was a sound from beyond the windows or perhaps the brush of some confused dream lightly waking him. As he tried to clear away the cobwebs of sleep, Rullie felt a presence beside the bed – fragile, ethereal. He knew someone was there gazing down at him in the indigo shadows of the small room. He did not feel threatened in any way, merely curious. As he listened, motionless, he opened his eyes slightly and saw the silhouette of a young girl beside his bed. It was her. He longed for nothing more than to reach out and touch her but, quelling the pounding of his heart, he continued to lie still as if to gain time. Not realising he was awake, she bent down and with a graceful ease ran her hand lightly as a feather over his dishevelled hair, his shoulders, the tips of his fingers, over and around as if drawing an invisible pattern. A sliver of moonlight shone into the room and he saw it fluttering briefly like a moth in the young girl's eyes. Rullie felt his world begin to reel. He then did the only thing possible, knowing afterwards nothing could ever be as it was. Turning onto his back he slowly sat up and stretched out his arms to her.

'Come to me. Don't be afraid,' he said quietly.

At first she appeared startled as if she had expected him to stay sleeping. With dark eyes that asked for everything she smiled shyly at him, not understanding what he said to her, nor being practised in the ways of love. She let her little pet bird fly to the window sill and then sat down on the bed beside him, the silken folds of her robe falling round her like the petals of a flower. She was tremulous, unsure. He cupped her upturned face in both his hands and cautiously and very softly kissed her.

'I have imagined this moment for the past two years,' he said, his voice barely audible. A murmur of desire escaped from the young girl as he bent her head back to trace the curve of her ear with his lips and kiss the hollow at the base of her slender throat.

She sat still and silent as Rullie undid the small buttons of her garment, slowly, carefully, one by one. The silk slipped off her smooth amber-coloured shoulders, over her small, perfect breasts, and fell like a discarded letter to the floor. He reached round the curve of her waist and with infinite tenderness laid the young girl back on the bed. She was trembling and as if in complete surrender one of her hands was folded like a dove's wing against his chest.

'You are so beautiful,' he whispered, holding her tightly to him and burying his face in her hair, a sea of flower-scented ebony fanning over the pillow like a halo.

He looked into her bewitching eyes then kissed their sweeping lashes with the surface of his lips, taking his time to reach her soft mouth once again. As they caressed one another a mutual gentle fire began to spread over them and each could hear the wild beating of the other's heart as they drifted into rapture.

At that moment Rullie, lost in the completeness of her willing body, felt himself clearly loving her above all else.

When he awoke at dawn she was gone. Rullie rose from his bed and searched for some sign of farewell. The atmosphere was filled with the despair of a lover left unexpectedly. The scent of the young girl lingered faintly in the room, luring him to a corner. There on a low table he found a small plant in a rough-hewn pot. It was wrapped in silk. He carefully removed the covering and found, nestled in the centre of several dark green waxy leaves, a single flower. Featherings of the palest rose fanned out like delicate sea coral from the base. The petals of the blossom were large and creamy-white with a dazzling luminosity. Each petal curved gently outwards as though innocently willing to offer up its secrets. The beauty of the flower was incomparable and the sensation of its perfume impossible to forget. Rullie knew instantly this must be the flowering plant to which MacLellan had referred.

Dwarfed by the plant on the table was a small jute bundle secured with a string. Once untied, dozens of apricot stones spilled out. In her haste, he thought the young girl had mistakenly left behind her little bird. It was perched on a wooden beam which stretched across the rafters of the ceiling. The bird was looking down at him, its eyes darting to and fro. Unable to reach it, Rullie gathered up the seeds and plant and hid them carefully among his belongings.

Just as he finished this task four armed men burst into the room. They tied Rullie's arms behind his back, blindfolded him and marched him past Cordell who appeared frozen in astonishment. Down through the dusty streets of the town with the pungent smell of horse manure seeping from the earth, and into the presence of Zafran Khan. One of his captors removed the blindfold and he was forced to kneel, his head bowed. The Mir observed him silently, with the distaste he reserved for stupid offenders. There was something terrifying and unutterable in the black pits of his eyes. He drew his dagger from its sheath hanging from his waist and, flicking his fingers against its metal edges to test its sharpness, he advanced towards Rullie. He trod as silently as a thief until his bare feet were directly under the downcast eyes of his prisoner.

'Your business was in Hunza, Englishman, not here. It seems you have forsaken your objectivity. Your ways are not ours and here foolishness can only result in death.'

His situation rendering him defenceless, Rullie kept silent. His only thought was of what may have befallen the young girl who had risked the wrath of both Allah and her father by loving an infidel. At the same time, he knew it was inconceivable that the Mir could imagine his daughter daring to visit a man outside the confines of marriage.

Zafran Khan walked round the kneeling figure and placed his hand on the nape of his captive's neck. Rullie waited for the blow that would end his life. With one quick thrust he felt the dagger slice through the rope binding his wrists and heard the calm voice of the ruler,

'Leave. If I ever see you again, I will kill you.'

Rullie returned to the house to collect his bags. He hurriedly placed the apricot stones and the small plant in the deep recesses of one of them. Cordell was nowhere to be seen. As he glanced around the bedroom he saw lying on the floor the little bird belonging to the young girl. Two of its feathers, the colour of amethyst, spiralled upwards in minute circles in the breeze. Its tiny neck, still warm, was broken.

He was escorted by three armed men as far as the border. They did not treat him harshly but so bruised was his heart that he hardly saw the world or the people in it. From Peshawar he chose a route that would take him to Rawalpindi and down through a string of villages whose warlike forefathers had once ridden north to conquer the disparate kingdoms of the high Himalayas. Wherever he could he bartered for seeds and filled his pockets with them. Two native collectors were added along the way and in densely covered hills he searched for further botanical riches, entering into a world of silence and gloom with little enthusiasm. Before breaking camp each dawn he made sure his unique, precious flowering plant was safe and secure.

On a crisp autumnal morning eleven days later he found a particularly rare example of Himalayan birch. The pale coppery-orange bark glimmered like a siren in the golden light. He climbed into the tree and shook the branches with all his strength, as if in some way to purge himself, until its seed fell onto the ground below. He filled his bags to the brim, took a few extra cuttings and continued on his way.

That night, writing his journal by lantern-light outside his tent while the Indian helpers were asleep some distance away, Rullie's anguish seemed limitless. Digging into his pocket he found the small lump of opium offered to him by the Afghans to cure his pain on the night he was stung by the scorpion. Curious to feel its effects one day, he had kept it. Turning it over several times in the palm of his hand he wondered if it might ease his dreadful torment. He took a little clay pipe bowl out of his bag, placed a drop of black substance onto the platform of the bowl and held it over a flame. As it started to bubble he drew the smoke deep into lungs until he felt a sense of calm – a euphoric, cloudless serenity that began to relieve him of his melancholy. Later looking up at the stars he found himself laughing quietly.

'Life is utterly insane.'

Further and further the heavenly demon drew him into its thrall until he felt himself almost drowning in a delicious, subtle dream-like trance which lasted many hours, until time and the future lost all meaning.

A fortnight later he reached Bombay where he carefully loaded his glazed cases filled with plants onto a steamboat which would travel round the Cape and on to England. He kept one case to carry home personally and boarded a boat bound for Arabia. After two weeks and four days on the high seas he stepped ashore. He travelled to Baghdad, crossed the Syrian desert in a camel caravan and, arriving in Alexandria, boarded a freighter which conveyed him to his homeland. Once in London, in a state of exhaustion, he travelled by train to Dorset and took a stage-coach home from the station. Carefully tucked into his breast pocket was a jade and gold bracelet beautifully crafted in Jaipur to give to Charlotte.

When Rullie reached the gates of Ashmore, he told the driver to stop. For a long while he gazed in silence down the drive at the rose-gold glow in the windows of his house. He counted each of them, one by one, as if to imprint on his mind all that was essential in his life. Opening his front door he saw Charlotte sitting by the fire reading. As always there was about her a certain grace, warm and comforting. As soon as she saw him she dropped her book to the floor and went quickly towards him, a smile on her pale lovely face. He encircled her waist with both hands and drew her into his embrace.

'I have been so worried about you,' Charlotte said, placing her head into the hollow of his neck. He held her tightly and fixed his eye on a spot on the wall opposite. 'I believed you might never return.'

Her husband smiled to reassure her and continued to hold her close for a minute or two. Then, lifting up her right hand, he carefully slipped the jade bracelet over her delicate wrist.

Just as one can never determine the exact truth, the intimate nature, of another's life, Rullie would never realise what had taken place in Charlotte's world during his absence. She never mentioned that she had once again been with child and four months after his departure, her perpetual anxiety had led to its loss. Nor how her bereavement deepened before she was able to come to terms with it in a gradual, unresolved way. She kept silent about the many hours spent in the chapel asking God for guidance and praying for the soul of her child, the safe deliverance of her husband.

She never told him that on returning from the chapel one day she had witnessed an astonishing scene, one which would remain with her always. On that cold misty morning she chanced upon a group of deer stepping silently out of a thicket into a field. In their midst she saw one that was unlike any she had seen before. It was pure white, luminous and exquisite. From afar she could almost believe it was a unicorn. She stood transfixed, staring at it until it eventually vanished, feeling somehow that it was a premonition, like an angel on her shoulder, and that her fortunes would soon change.

Instead, Charlotte showed her husband all the attention women give to those who have endured hardships in lands on the other side of the world. In the evenings she sat beside him, once again entranced by his stories and so as not to perturb him, talked lightly of her own days.

Naturally, one of his first friends to see the flowering plant was MacLellan.

'I take my hat off to you, my friend. What an absolute gem. I always thought it might have been a myth. Now tell me all about it. Where on earth did you find it?' he bellowed in his excitement. Skirting around the subject by extolling the beauty of Hunza's mountain flowers, all Rullie would say as to how he came upon it was that the circumstances had been unusual.

'There is only this one. I could find no others,' he eventually said.

Ten days after he arrived home he set off for London once again. This time for Kew and to await the arrival of his plants from India. In his arms he carried his little plant. It seemed as though the foliage would burst from its clay pot. Sir William Hooker, who continued to teach Rullie much about practical botany when time allowed, examined it with meticulous care. He pored over the field notes and dried plant material, drawings and watercolour sketches of the blossom done by the plant hunter, before calling in various experts who were equally astonished by its exceptional quality. After two unnerving weeks for the man who had found it, the plant was declared an entirely new genus and was named 'Montrosia Fragans' in the botanist's honour.

'Congratulations, Rullie Montrose, this is a triumph for you. Perhaps you will make your fortune after all,' the director smiled, as he clapped his friend on the back.

The only stipulation made by Rullie, since the expedition had been at his sole expense, was his wish to keep the plant in his possession. He was prepared to sell Kew the seeds only.

'No problem, no problem at all,' said Sir William.

One morning after his return the couple were walking around the glasshouse together when Charlotte stopped and pointed to his new plant. It had by now spent its flowering, its seeds set but not dispersed.

'What exactly is it?' she asked.

'It has no name.'

'How strange to find such a pretty flower in such a harsh, violent country.'

'I suppose it is.'

'Are you particularly fond of it?'

Her husband kept his eyes fastened on the tips of the leaves.

'Only once or twice in a lifetime do you come across such a beauty. But all flowers are fleeting, ephemeral things. They are like clouds, like children. They change shape and drift away. Shall we continue our walk?'

Rullie spent the months that preceded winter immersed in the soothing rhythms and rituals of the country. Nature was his solace and in it he found a faith usually the preserve of the Church. He sought a perfect spot for his flowering plant near the stream where it would be planted out next spring once it had gained in strength and hardiness from the warmth of a well-stocked glasshouse in winter.

He encouraged his small young apricot tree which had spread its branches and reached an agreeable height in his absence. He made certain that dozens of new apricot seeds were placed in the correct amount of potting soil and suitable compost in their little clay pots with even more care than usual. He conferred continually with Gibbes under whose wing in his absence the restoration of order had been superbly managed. It had been a bad year for the villagers whose lives more often than not turned on a sixpence. Many were of the opinion that if it hadn't been for work provided by the estate following the storm their tables would have been bare of bread and the sufferings of their children unimaginable.

Rullie wandered round the arboretum and took comfort in the company of his trees, enjoying the strong, distinct personalities of each. As the snow cast a protective cloak over the land, he felt their uncomplaining trunks, the starkness of their bare bones, all as necessary to him as a trickle of water to a thirsty man.

And wherever he went from morning until night his conscience followed him – a sharp, clear persistent echo.

Charlotte awoke each morning to the pleasure of her husband being beside her. But little by little as the days slipped by she sensed that he was suffering from some deep malaise. He did not rise early as was his usual habit. Instead he lay back upon their feathered bed, his eyes searching the grey skies through the windows. Her intuition told her something calamitous had befallen him. Something irrevocable which could change the ordered pattern of their lives. Although he clearly appreciated even her smallest gesture of affection, he remained apart as if musing upon an abstraction.

One day, pitying her own confusion and wanting nothing more than to peel away his layer of reticence until she found a simple truth, she caught herself stifling a sob.

'Dearest husband, what has caused you such unhappiness?' Her words were full of tender anxious concern. But Rullie, who dearly loved his wife, knew he could never divulge the secret agony of his soul.

'It's nothing, absolutely nothing. Really.'

And so for the first time in their marriage Charlotte became guarded in her dealings with her husband. She kept her thoughts to herself and struggled to keep hidden any welling resentment. In time-honoured fashion she waited patiently for the day he would return to her and they could resume their life as before. Only MacLellan, who over the years had grown to adore Charlotte, noticed the lack of sparkle in her eyes.

Exactly three months after his return Rullie sat down opposite MacLellan at The Friar's Tuck. It was, as usual, a Thursday at seven o'clock. The night was dark as ink and a cold, drenching rain beat down like silver needles upon Wexton Abbas. Never has a man looked so riven, thought MacLellan, as he gazed affectionately at his friend. 'What a bloody miserable night,' he said instead, shaking the drops from his coat. The two men stayed near the fire while Symonds the tavern owner placed before them a couple of cigars newly imported from Havana and two pewter tankards. MacLellan took a long, slow draught, so slowly that Rullie's eyes were fixed upon the movement of his swallowing. The Scotsman came straight to the point.

'There is about you a sadness which is unusual, not to say unfortunate. You'd feel better if you spoke of what bothers you.' He was not a man who usually pried but he just couldn't bear to witness the unhappiness of others. The long silence that followed was accompanied by the background banter of working men genial with drink. Rullie stifled an impulse to stand up and leave. Instead, not wishing to cause offence, he leant forward in his chair, his elbows on the table and after taking a deep breath he softened and said, 'I met a young girl in Hunza.'

'Go on.'

'When I was first there she came into the room wearing a garment of the palest green, which floated like gossamer as she walked across the floor. She had almond-shaped eyes, almost golden, and loose hair reaching below the small of her back.'

He felt as if he were shouting in a dream.

For an hour he talked. And for an hour MacLellan listened motionless. His ale lay untouched. The ash from his cigar had dropped into a cold pile on the table, like a tiny, dormant volcano. Then Rullie said quietly, 'At times I find the pain of coping with her absence unbearable.'

Silence.

He looked down at his hands which were clenched tightly together and said after a while, 'I never even knew her name. The thought of never seeing her again brings a piercing desolation.'

MacLellan's eyes brimmed with moisture though it might have been the smoke from the fire making his eyes smart.

'That's the thing about passion and loss,' he said, as calmly as he could. 'In its throes, and I should know, all reason flies out of the window.' As if ruminating on past adventures, he sighed and shook his head. The two men drained the dregs of their tankards as Symonds passed by. He overheard MacLellan muttering, 'A chap needs to be alone when his heart is broken,' and wondered what he was on about.

Rullie and the Scotsman left the tavern and walked silently together to the gates of the estate, each dwelling upon the complexities of human longing. As he said good-night, MacLellan offered a few final words of advice.

'Forget the temptation to run back to her, my friend. The echoes will fade and you will recover.' They both looked at the lights of the cottage which shimmered like fireflies caught in amber.

'Perhaps,' said Rullie softly as he turned into the driveway.

The year was 1859. The year that Charles Darwin, once a young vigorous field naturalist, published a book explaining his theory of evolution which was enthusiastically embraced by the public. By then his friend Joseph Hooker, son of Sir William and a plant hunter famous for collecting many sumptuous rhododendrons from Sikkim in the Himalayas, had become one of his closest confidants.

Nearly four thousand miles away, as British troops took Baluchistan, leaving Afghanistan completely landlocked and thus effectively closing off India to the growing Russian Empire, South America was offering up a myriad of hidden botanical novelties to the world.

And for some inexplicable reason there was a rain of tiny fish over England.

Rullie made it known to both Kew and Veitch that due to the pressure of work on the estate he would prefer not to travel to the other side of the world that year. Instead he came to an arrangement with the latter, not particularly lucrative it must be said, to embark on an investigation of the mountains of Smyrna, an important centre of botanical exploration for the past four hundred years. He was to stay in Turkish villages which were filthy and offered only bad bread, onions and sour milk to eat. But none of this did he embark on before his flowering plant had once again been successfully nurtured into blossom. Nor before several of the tender apricot saplings

131

were replanted along the lengthy back brick wall to which the glasshouse was attached. He told Gibbes he wished their arms to be trained and pruned in the espalier fashion eventually. This he hoped, when laden with fruit, would be close to horti-cultural perfection.

For the first time in many years he returned towards the end of June when the heavy scent of lime flowers still hung in the air. The following month he took his wife to Paris for two weeks where they visited the usual sights and in a small shop in the Rue de la Paix he brought her a dress of the finest oyster silk. Early each morning they strolled in the Bois de Bologne, observing the elegant riders and conjurers who made them laugh with their antics. Each evening they dined in a different restaurant and after feeling the beguiling effects of wine, they would retire to their room and let their interrupted love wash over them. Both admitting to an unexpected happiness, they returned home with renewed optimism and settled into a routine of concord and serenity which had recently been missing from their lives.

Rullie gradually assumed the air of one at peace with himself. He neither sought nor evaded any mention of Hunza. Although the memories of his painful interlude remained, he managed to suppress any nostalgia for the wholeness once within his grasp. It was as though a calm blue lake had covered over that brief enchanted moment and he was thus able to endure, unaltered, the same steadiness of days he had led before his fatal trip. The villagers, who were fond of him, felt relieved all was tranquil again in his house and an air of contentment spread like a protective cloak over Wexton Abbas. Rullie was considerate to all he came across and asked for nothing more than to care for his land and his wife. If he played poker with MacLellan with the passion of a convert and occasionally could be heard singing too loudly as he staggered home with his arm around his friend after one too many pints of ale, that was only to be expected from a man who spent half his life in the dark pagan recesses of the world.

When sadness came upon him – as sometimes happened on a Sunday – he submitted to a curious indulgence. Accompanied by his dog he would walk past the delicate flowering plant and sit beneath his favourite beech tree. A lichen-encrusted niche between the giant's feet offered a perfect repose and many years of feeling its rounded hollow had worn a soft burrow for him. For hours he lay back, listening to the music of the natural world and looking up at the sky between the vault of green. For he imagined he saw there in the pools of light dancing between the leaves all the mystery of his life. Once the convolutions of thought were soothed he felt reassured that in the land in which he was born man and tree could not survive, one without the other.

In July he received a letter from Allegra asking him to visit her. He told his wife he had business at the coast and would be back the following day. He had not seen Allegra for over two years and when he arrived he was pleased to see she still shared her patch of land with sea eagles and otters. Wild dog roses clambered up the steps to her garish caravan and dandelions dotted the grass beneath his feet. Nothing appeared to have changed.

Allegra opened the door dressed in a black robe, almost transparent and embroidered with large red flowers. As she bent down to kiss him the fold of her robe fell open slightly and he noticed the swell of her breast was sallow, no longer warm or inviting.

'Are you still chasing your dreams, Rullie Montrose?' she asked with a wan smile, wiping her brow in a somewhat listless fashion. Rullie saw immediately that she was not well. Her arms were thin and her once lustrous hair, the colour of a raven's wing, lay dank and lifeless. Dark blue shadows filled the circles under her eyes. Once he had gathered his wits he saw peeking out from behind her robe a young boy with sea-green eyes and a mop of pale gold curls which sprang like a sunburst around him.

'This is my son,' said Allegra simply.

Rullie fought to hide his surprise.

'What is your name?' he said, crouching down so that his eyes were on a level with the boy's.

'Alexis.'

Allegra seemed on the point of saying something. Instead she gathered up her child and placed him on her hip. Then she beckoned to Rullie Montrose to follow her outside. While the boy and the small dog ran across the field, Rullie and Allegra sat on grass carpeted with tufts of moss and clover and for a while watched them play. Fine feathers of clouds passed overhead. Allegra took her old friend's hand and said, 'I am ill. I have no family to turn to and must ask for your help. When the time comes I would like him to live with you.'

Silence fell, only broken by the child's small cries of delight as he chased a seagull. It was difficult not to ache for the chirpy-looking little boy who, without his mother, would tumble into the world without much comfort or hope.

'Who is his father?' asked Rullie.

'It is of no consequence. He left as soon as he knew I was with child.'

Allegra sighed. 'It was in his nature to hurt the innocent.'

'I will make sure you are both cared for. I will talk to my wife.'

Rullie left later that night and stayed at an inn near the sea so that the sound of the surf falling on the shore might erase any thought of the suffering Alexis would one day endure.

In the spring of the following year when the trees were in new leaf and his mother had died, Alexis came to live with Rullie Montrose and his wife. Since Charlotte had heard her husband frequently mention his old friend throughout the years, it was within her circuit of compassion to understand the need for this. In a short time he became the light of her life and filled the days while her husband was away with all the joy a woman might expect from a child of her own. She showed him the lairs of foxes and in winter took him to watch the coppicing of hazelnut trees, the wood from which were made hurdles for shepherds. Slowly over time she introduced him to the ways of the village children.

It was the villagers' belief that an abundance of poppies scattered round their cornfields would ensure them of a bountiful harvest. The flowers also provided a small income to help them make ends meet. In the long shimmering days of July when the corn was ripening, Alexis, trailing his butterfly net, eagerly followed the children into the ruffled fields. Early each morning, for not a farthing's gain, girls and boys of all ages were sent out with muslin bags hanging limply round their necks. These they were obliged to fill to the brim with scarlet petals as quickly as their little hands were able. Once full they ran back through the fields to the village. There they stood silently watching the villagers rapidly pack the petals in straw and send them off to market before they could wilt and fade, the dark red syrup extracted to be used for the sick and

the infirm. Alexis was a strong, good-natured little boy but when tired of the older children, he would wander off to seek out the tell-tale crimson of wild strawberries or forage for mushrooms hidden among ribbons of grass.

In 1865, on the opposite side of the world, the Civil War in America was drawing to its bloody and bitter close. Slavery was abolished and shortly afterwards Abraham Lincoln was dead, assassinated while attending a theatre performance. That same year Rullie found sufficient cause to return to Asia – to the beautiful island of Ceylon

In the delicate land of rainforests hung with orchids and mountain slopes carpeted with ferns, he spent two months collecting bulbs. But he failed to secure those of a rare orchid possessing amber petals and a striking orange-brown lip, which were pinned high on the shoulder of a wet, slippery hill. Much to his annoyance he found another plant hunter methodically harvesting his chosen patch, a surly individual known to destroy all the wild orchids he was unable to transport in order to preserve their rarity. And as the rules of the game demanded, Rullie was forced to leave empty-handed.

He arrived home in the second week of August.

At twilight, as the swallows winged their way back to their resting places.

On the path leading to his cottage he found a horse loosely tethered to a tree. Inside he found his wife playing the piano, her beautiful hands reaching over the keys as she concentrated on a Brahms sonata. Next to the fire sat an older man listening to the glorious melody, his eyes fixed on her with open admiration. Rullie noticed as she finished playing Charlotte smiled at her guest, then, blushing, filled the room with the most delightful of laughs. When she saw her husband she rose quickly to greet him. She felt a happiness flood over her as he held her in his embrace.

'This gentleman has travelled many miles to see you,' she said as she released herself. 'He is also a plant hunter of whom I feel sure you have heard.'

'I have recently been in the Himalayas,' said the man, rising to his feet. 'I heard your name mentioned more than once and felt I must meet you.' His name was James Lanson, a man renowned for his tenacity in his field. As a young man he had accompanied David Douglas, the famous plant hunter after whom the fir was named, to the Sandwich Islands.

'I was boring your wife with my gruesome stories,' he laughed, glancing at Charlotte. 'We were chatting about poor Douglas. Not many collectors – ravenously hungry in the North American wilderness – twice have to eat their own horse to survive.'

After a short interval he continued with his memories. 'But the day he died is firmly etched on my mind. One day out collecting in the Islands he fell into a pit-trap and was gored to death, his body found under a snorting wild bull. What a waste. He was only thirty-five,' he observed, as if it had happened only yesterday.

After an early dinner the two men walked outside where a sweet golden light played over the garden. For many hours they talked of their travels. 'I went up to Hunza, that land of gold and apricots. What an extraordinary place,' said Lanson.

'Yes, fascinating, isn't it.' Rullie showed not the slightest alteration in his voice. His guest continued his story.

'An old Frenchman there told me a strange story. Rather poignant, really. It appears that seven years ago a young girl – the daughter of the Mir – who was betrothed to another, fell in love with a visiting Englishman. Apparently it was an overwhelming but fatal affair. Unbeknown to her father the two lovers had been together on the eve of her marriage. When he found out three months after the man's departure that his unhappy daughter was with child her fate was sealed. From his point of view she had deliberately ensured the dishonour of her family and he showed little clemency. She was taken blindfolded into a glade in a forest where she was made to kneel. With one swift blow, she was beheaded, a sword slicing easily through her slender young neck. Her broken body was left there for the buzzards.'

He paused before concluding, 'Ah, love like that is tempestuous and irresistible, don't you think?'

Rullie felt his heart shatter in thousand pieces. The colour drained from his face and his legs became as heavy as lead.

He could say nothing. He excused himself as politely as he could, told Charlotte he wished to sit with Alexis while he slept, and like an old man with eyes staring into the distance of his past, walked slowly up the stairs.

143

Within a few weeks the health of Rullie Montrose began to decline. There appeared to be no reason. Only he knew that since hearing of the death of the young girl he had lost some vital part of himself. He found it difficult to acknowledge the changes to his body and spirit and so refused to alter either his habits or routine.

In late summer the original apricot tree was, for the first time, heavily laden with swelling fruit. Its abundance was astonishing. Hanging from the slender branches were four hundred apricots. Perfect golden yellow orbs, each possessing a sweetness like nectar. The children from the village came to wonder. It was a cause for celebration and Charlotte delighted in preparing a banquet for all the inhabitants of Wexton Abbas. Botanists and in particular fruiterers, having heard of its marvellous properties, came from all over to admire the tree for themselves and to bite into its succulent, sun-warmed fruit. It was therefore safely assumed the following year would see the blossoming of the third batch of trees, which in turn would enrich the pockets of all involved.

Rullie did not leave England in the spring, preferring to be near his wife and Alexis. In his arboretum was everything nostalgia ordered. The flowering plant from Hunza, from which he derived a not inconsiderable income, remained a slender pale-eyed beauty, its sublime blossom and perfume unsurpassed in any corner of the country.

Joseph Hooker had by now succeeded his father Sir William as director of Kew and he and Rullie made a habit of meeting once a month in London. Evenings with MacLellan were seldom neglected and on Saturdays Alexis would twist his father's arm to take him to the fair on the village green. Sundays were devoted to his wife when they would walk down country lanes and through the surrounding fields, extolling the virtues of this plant or that. Listening together in the garden to the evening song of the blackbird sitting on his chimney-pot, he felt a familiar safety and comfort in her presence.

By the end of May Rullie felt increasingly unwell. One day he asked Charlotte to accompany him to the great beech in the parkland. They sat together until the shadows lengthened and the sun disappeared behind the distant hills. Looking up through the grey-green branches at the banks of clouds racing across the darkening sky, he saw there clearly the varying milestones of his life and felt at peace.

That evening Rullie caught a slight fever. He kissed his wife and Alexis good-night and retired to bed early. In the midnight hour, with Charlotte lying beside him, he suddenly sat up and called out her name. As he fell back upon the pillow she clutched his limp hand to her heart. A few minutes later he gave a small sigh and died. The doctors declared that his heart had simply given out. All the years of hard travel had perhaps finally taken their toll. A distraught MacLellan had his own thoughts as to the reason why.

All were saddened by his death. He had been a man incapable of malice, at the age of forty-eight in the prime of his life, and generous to many. Some of the villagers even wondered what their futures might hold. Men, women and children from Wexton Abbas turned up at the family chapel to say their final farewells. Led by Charlotte and MacLellan, whose emotions were not entirely in control, they accompanied his coffin back up the avenue of ancient yews to the gravesite. Rullie had instructed in his will that his body was not to be placed in the family vault. He wished instead to be buried next to his infant daughter at the foot of the giant Cedar of Lebanon.

Once the ceremony was completed, his widow thanked everyone for their kindness and with her arm around young Alexis, returned home. To grieve and learn to come to terms with the death of the man she loved.

Following her loss, Charlotte's life felt like a lonelier continuation of their years together, though by necessity a more decisive and involved one. Her principal aspiration, apart from nurturing Alexis, was to persevere with the life's work of her husband. She felt required to ensure the survival of all he had created, in particular his arboretum and his apricot trees which by now had gained a solid reputation, with every appearance of enthusiasm. In order to achieve this, however, she needed to make one slight alteration to his carefully laid plans.

Six weeks after his funeral, early one morning before the world was awake, she took the largest knife in the house and walked down towards the stream, meandering between the trees until she stood in front of what she was looking for. Bending down, she angled the heavy implement and with three swift strokes sliced cleanly through the thick green stem of the ravishing flowering plant Rullie had brought back from his travels to Hunza.

The one on which he had poured such boundless and intimate care.

Lying on the ground at her feet were four large creamy-white flowers, like a flock of doves felled in mid-flight. Each perfect petal still curved gently outwards, offering an illusion of simplicity. The flower's hypnotic perfume, always so exquisite, faded rapidly, almost at the very moment of its demise.

Once Charlotte had completed her task she picked up one of the flowers from its severed stem. Cradling it in the palm of her right hand, she walked the short distance to the tree beneath which her husband's body lay. She carefully placed the large delicate blossom on top of the newly dug grave. After a brief moment of reflection she turned slowly round and with a renewed sense of peace and purpose walked with small firm steps back to her cottage.

Thanks to

Claire Clifton, my friend, for her invaluable
advice,editorial expertise and tireless help.
My daughter, Tara, for her patience
in suggesting various subtle changes and
my other daughter, Tasmin, for all her
encouragement. Thanks must also go to
all those writers who have written fascinating,
informative books on trees and flowering
plants from which I learned so much.